Praise for the On Call stories:

On Call: Afternoon

The plotting is gentle with the focus very much on the relationship. I liked this and very much enjoyed this strong character based story.

~ Jenre's Well Read

This is only a short story but it's very nice and romantic, and how could be anything else, when we are speaking of hot doctors and their furry friends, little matchmaker kitties?

~Elisa Rolle

On Call: Dancing

The On Calls short stories are both really nice, and I would suggest to read them together, or at least at short distance.

~Elisa Rolle

On Call: Crossroads

There is a lot that happens in this story, but the end, well suffice it to say that I still get a little teary-eyed... but all in a good—*very,* **very** good—way.

~Blackraven's Reviews

Tough subjects are dealt with sensitively and the sweet, honest couple of men at the core of the story trying to make sense of their relationship and the world provided a satisfying read.

~Literary Nymphs

Also by P.D. Singer

Novels
    The Rare Event
    Spokes
    Fire on the Mountain
    Snow on the Mountain
    Fall Down the Mountain
    Blood on the Mountain
    Return to the Mountain

    Coming Soon: A New Man

Novellas
    Donal *agus* Jimmy

Shorts
    Cross the Mountain
    Prep Work
    O'Carolan's Seduction
    On Call: Afternoon
    On Call: Dancing
    On Call: Crossroads
    Training Cats
    Tail Slide (Also available as Slip/Slide/Snow in the *Out in Colorado* anthology)

ON CALL

THE COLLECTION

P.D. SINGER

ROCKY RIDGE BOOKS

ISBN-13 978-1-62622-020-1

ON CALL

THE COLLECTION

P.D. SINGER

Contents

On Call: Afternoon

"Exam Room Three, Dr. Hoyer," Michelle told me as she handed the chart over. "He hasn't been in before, and he's kind of jumpy. He seems to know enough to be dangerous, too—he's got the medical terminology down pat."

Patients with knowledge could be a blessing or a curse. I looked through the chart quickly, wanting to be prepared before walking into my first appointment of what would be a busy day. "He's had a lot of the same training I've had, no wonder he slings the lingo. He's a veterinarian and he has to know a dozen species' worth. I only have to know humans." Michelle blushed, caught out in not reading thoroughly, something she wouldn't do again—she was too good a nurse for that. We'd been sizing each other up in the weeks since I'd joined the practice and mutual respect was growing.

It was still mixed in with a bit of romantic speculation: would the new (young, single) doctor want to date any of the staff? Well, no, not even if I was new in town and didn't know anyone else, but certainly I didn't want to mess with a functioning office. There had been a few offers to set me up with girlfriends, which I'd turned down as well. No one had offered to introduce me to possible boyfriends. A pity. I had few illusions about my own attractiveness: medium height, medium build, medium light brown hair, medium handsome all paled before the MD after my name for most people. I could probably be Dr. Toad and still get dates with some of them. I worked out a lot of my frustrations on that score at the gym.

I took another quick look through the history before stepping through the door: single black male, thirty-four, intermittent fever, malaise, a swollen lymph node (patient's description). Could be a lot of things.

"Hello, I'm Dr. Keith Hoyer." Putting a hand out to a patient dressed in a backless gown without a twitch was one of those skills you gain early in a medical career. Good thing, too, because patients can provoke a reaction for a lot of different reasons—usually not because they are drop-dead gorgeous. Like this guy. My mouth went dry as he shook my hand and introduced himself.

"Dante James." The name hung well on the handsome man, who sat straight backed on the end of the examining table, his espresso legs showing bare from the hem of the gown.

"Shouldn't that be Dr. James?" I found my voice again.

"If I'm the one in a backless gown, I don't think I'll be insisting on the 'Doctor' part. I have a small animal practice here in town." His hand had been warm in mine; now it lay in his lap again. "But Dr. James or Dante will do."

"So you have to work without your patients telling you directly what's the matter." We exchanged a grin of understanding; pediatric patients had some of the same challenges. I liked adults. "Why don't you tell me what brings you in?"

"I've been having a mild fever off and on, generally not feeling well, but I figured that was probably self limiting, until this lymph node blew up. It hurts." He met my eyes calmly, which I did my best to match. I made a note in the chart.

"Where is the lymph node?" *Please let it be somewhere neutral.*

"My groin."

I set the chart down, adjusting my attitude to "professional." "Let's check it out." If I listened to his heart and lungs first I could manage myself better—I hoped.

He scooted back on the exam table and let me lift the end up under his legs. When he tried to lie back, he winced, so I supported him enough to land without a flop. His liver and spleen weren't enlarged, though if I imagined my pale hand against his dark skin under the gown as I determined this, there would be enlargement elsewhere. I bit the inside of my cheek as a preventive measure.

"Just on the one side, or have you noticed lymph nodes enlarging on both sides?" I asked, as I lifted the gown above his hips. He still had his cotton boxers on; my hand could slide under and I could leave them there.

"Just the one side." He hissed when I found the node; he was correct in his identification and it was huge, easily the size of a walnut. A few flanking nodes were enlarged, too, but not nearly as much. Just to the left of his package, they were clearly palpable under the skin of his lean body. I had to check the other side, just to be sure. To do that, I had to move his genitalia away, pushing with the side of my hand to allow my fingertips

3

access to the nodes. Even with the soft fabric between my hand and his body, I wanted to react. He had closed his eyes and was breathing evenly.

"Have any of your patients scratched you recently?" I was proud of myself; that had come out normally.

"All the time." He held out his arms, decorated with a fine network of lines in different stages of healing.

"Glad my patients don't do that to me." I had been mauled once or twice. "How about on your lower body?"

"One cat ran right down my leg a few weeks ago." He pulled the gown up farther to show me the pinkish, nearly-healed tracks on his thigh. What a shame that smooth skin got marked. "It healed oddly, little papules for a while."

"Well, I believe you have a dandy case of cat scratch fever," I told him. "They do warn you about this in vet school?"

"Yes, though they don't mention what a lymph node in your groin an inch and a half across feels like. I totter around like an old man." He shook his head, his closely clipped hair making a little rasping sound against the protective paper cover on the table. "I did think it was nothing but that, and yet..."

"Yes?" I prompted him when he stopped talking to stare at the ceiling.

"It's possible that, well..." Now he looked me straight on. "Let's just say I got a bit crazy about six months ago, and I've been wondering about my HIV status since."

"We can run a test anonymously, just to set your mind at ease." I patted his arm; I'd sweated out the same thing. "But I really do think it's cat scratch fever. Stay put, I'll get the phlebotomy things and do this myself."

"Thanks," he said, as I slipped out the door.

I couldn't keep treating him. Today, but not again. No matter how the blood work came back. It just wasn't ethical to date patients.

He lay quietly as the blood welled into the little vial. The paperwork would call him #3187. I wondered what I'd say when I called him with the results. Then I wondered what he'd say when I called to relinquish his care to someone else in the practice, and ask him to dinner.

"That's it, aside from that lymph node. I can drain it, just so you can move around again."

"That would be good. I had to fish a cat from under the exam table and I thought I was going to be stuck down there with it yesterday." His chuckle was wry.

"As long as I don't have to fish you out from under the table when you see the size of the needle I'm going to stick you with." He was going to have to take his boxers down for me to do that. I tamped "professional" on my face a little harder as I pulled things out of drawers.

"You probably don't want to watch this," I suggested as I returned with my armory—a wide bore needle on a big syringe without its barrel and an alcohol wipe.

"Probably not. Funny, I can do surgery on a cat but I can't watch you stick me." He turned to the wall after sliding his boxers down around his thighs, so he missed my face as I saw him revealed and also the medical show that left him sighing in relief as the node deflated. The little round peach bandage showed pale against his skin.

"That's a lot better. The other nodes aren't nearly that bad." He pulled up his boxers and sat up, far more easily than he'd lain down. The gown dropped back into his lap.

"I'll call you when the lab work comes back. It could be two days, it could be a week." I turned to dispose of the medical waste before looking at him again. "But I really think the cat scratch would have made you a lot sicker than you've described if you were positive." I wrote out a prescription for an antibiotic and ripped it off the pad.

"I'm going to hold on to that thought," Dante said as he took the script. "Because it's going to be a long few days as it is."

Yes, it is, I thought as I picked up another chart, preparing to treat some stomach ailment in the next room. Because I'm going to spend it thinking about how his thick dark cock looked as it lay against his curly pubic hair, and what I could do to coax it erect.

It was three days later that I picked up the phone. Dante thanked me graciously for the good news, and never had the chance to say yes or no to a dinner date. I had to end the call when all the other things I'd wanted to say stuck in my throat. He'd said he'd gotten crazy, he hadn't said how, and the uncertainty choked everything else; I couldn't know if he'd gotten crazy with another man. It would take some getting to know him first before I could offer the hands-on lesson in safe sex that I wanted so badly to give.

Weekends on call really suck canal water. A dateless Saturday night, as if that was unusual, although it was seriously busy. Why do babies wait until two A.M.? I'd spent a big chunk of the night delivering a little girl, and then had an admission to the hospital for an older man with chest pains. At least I was already there. A family practice had sounded a lot more enticing before they handed me the pager. It was around ten on Sunday morning before I staggered home for a few hours of sleep.

Someone would be glad to see me when I got home, not only because the hand that holds the can opener rules the world. Harpo, my big gray tabby cat, would greet me at the door most days unless the furnace was going, in which case I'd find him spreading his furry butt over a vent and stealing all the warmth. He'd seen me through medical school and internship, and had patiently waited through days of being alone or nearly so. Maybe not so patiently—he'd find something to destroy if it went on too long.

He'd sent one lover packing and been the sticking point for one or two others. Allergies can't be helped, I guess, but he'd managed to intimidate my one and only live-in boyfriend out in less than a month. With a creepy combination of relentless staring and cat pee, Harpo had convinced him to pack up and move out. I'd say that he took my credit card with him, but looking at the dates on the charges later, he'd been at it a bit longer than that. Old Harpo had a better handle on whom to trust than I did.

He did his dangerous ankle strop as he led me toward the empty dish, buzzing all the way. Kibbles and half a can of wet glop anchored him in the kitchen. I threw a frozen burrito in the microwave and headed to the shower, then dressed in some soft workout pants and a T-shirt. I managed to eat the burrito before I fell over, fully clothed, on the couch. If I went to bed I might never wake up for the next emergency.

Sometime later, I became vaguely aware of little peg feet marching across my stomach to my thighs, where a large warm weight flopped down on my groin. Nothing subtle about old Harpo; some cats might pussyfoot, but not this one. He might be part elephant but he was cuddly and my lap was his preferred spot. I drifted back to sleep.

When the pager went off again, it caught me in that weird state of waking that's disoriented but full of adrenaline. The beeping and buzzing startled Harpo, too, and I got a lap full of claws as he skedaddled and I flew off the couch trying to figure out what was going on. I did put one of my big feet right on the cat—his screech was the final stimulus to make me drop the pager and phone both. Harpo shot under the chair, hissing and yowling. I could answer my page or find out what I'd done to my cat. Trying to get him out from under the chair convinced me that I was better off with my pager, since he wasn't calm enough to touch and wouldn't be for a while. I stuck my bloody hand in my mouth and dialed the answering service.

"Hello, this is Dr. Hoyer. What seems to be the matter?" The answering service had put me through to the caller, a Mrs. Vincenza.

"My son Joey, he's three, fell off a chair and now he's holding his arm funny and crying..."

I led her through enough history to have a very good idea of what had happened and what to do about it. "Mrs. Vincenza, we can take care of this right away." I thought fast. "Where are you?" I could drag them into the office three miles from my wounded cat, or show up on her doorstep if that would be faster. Fortunately, she was less than a mile distant, so the sooner I reduced little Joey's subluxed elbow, the sooner I could do something about Harpo. "I'll be there in a few minutes."

It really does take extraordinary circumstances to get a doctor to make a house call these days, I thought, as I took one last look under the chair into baleful yellow eyes. "I'll be back for you, pal." He hissed—maybe that was what he was afraid of.

I could only hope that my cat had suffered no worse than little Joey had; I flexed and twisted his elbow enough that the ligament that had slipped into the joint when he'd fallen on the arm slipped back into its correct position. "See, Mrs. Vincenza, it wasn't really a broken wrist. They just hold their arms like that in nursemaid's elbow. He's fine now." The child moved his arm in wonder a few times and then ran off to play, skidding into a pile of blocks.

With thanks and backward glances toward her son, she let me out. She'd reached me on a Sunday—could I reach a vet if I needed to? Which vet? There was only one whose number I knew.

Harpo was still unwilling to come out from under the chair when I arrived home, a problem solved by picking the chair up off of him. "I need to check this out, pal. I don't know what I did to you." He'd calmed down a little, enough to let me hold him, but he swatted and hissed again as I found the joint in his hind leg that wasn't moving correctly. "I'm sorry, Harpo, I didn't mean to put my big foot on you. I think we need some help here."

He stayed on my lap as I dialed the number I'd used the other day, hoping that I could reach Dante James on a weekend. To my great relief, he answered on the second ring, though not with a professional greeting. He'd given me his private line; I should have realized.

"Hello, Dr. James? This is Keith Hoyer. I'm really sorry to bother you on a weekend, but I and my cat have a problem..." This time it was I who was coaxed through a history.

"Don't worry about disturbing me, Dr. Hoyer. I think you were right to be concerned. Can you bring Groucho, oh, sorry, Harpo, in? I'll be there; I live over the office."

"I can be there in about ten minutes once I get him into the carrier; that's going to be a task." He chuckled, making me chuckle, too. "It always is."

I use a carrier meant for a medium sized dog, because Harpo has legs the length of a giraffe's that telescope out for the express purpose of keeping him out of carriers. Oddly enough, his injury helped, because I could manage his front legs alone and got him into the box with only three curse words and one scratch. He glared at me some more, and once in the car I got a deep-chested growl. "Sorry, buddy, we're getting you to help." "Groucho" was the right name this time.

Dante's clinic was a two story house just off a main artery where the front door opened into a pleasant waiting area with a Plexiglas cat cage in one corner. A black and white tuxedo cat sat on a perch inside; the signs on the glass suggested that I should adopt it. The door had triggered a bell, which was followed by footsteps. Dante came around the corner. I was glad to see him, but there was a distinctly science-fictiony aspect to his appearance.

"Uh, what's moving under your shirt?" I stared in spite of myself.

Dante laughed and stroked the tail that stuck out at the neckline of the blue scrubs tops he wore over a T-shirt. It disappeared and was replaced by a small head with black and white stripes. "This is Mandy—

10

she's a sugar glider. They adore riding around inside people's clothes." He stroked her with one finger as she chittered madly at me and then ducked back into the scrubs. "I'm surprised she's awake. They're nocturnal."

The yawn caught me by surprise. "I'm beginning to think I'm nocturnal, too. I was up all night at the hospital." Maybe if I looked at him too long or wrong he'd chalk it up to tiredness.

"Poor guy. I know how that goes," Dante said as he led me to an exam room. He had a really nice ass, which I watched shamelessly since the opportunity presented itself. Harpo grumbled from his box, and then hissed when we tried to get him out. The open door didn't tempt him.

"I'll just take the top off," I suggested, not wanting to jostle his leg unnecessarily. Harpo went flat on the bottom, but Dante scooped him gently out and set him on the table. "Tell me what you need for help."

"Just hold him," the vet said, all attention on his patient. "He's guarding that hind leg." With gentle hands and soothing comments, Dante felt the leg thoroughly, dodging the one swipe Harpo took at him. "Yes, that hurt, and I know why." He let go; my cat tried to huddle against me. I snuggled him as Dante delivered the bad news. "The stifle joint is dislocated. Unfortunately, with cats that usually means a ruptured ligament or two. It's a surgical repair."

My heart sank. "I'm so sorry I stepped on you, buddy. So, when can you do it?"

Dante shrugged. "If you're willing to help I can do it now. I'd rather not wait, because he's in pain. He's not going to be getting from the litter box to the bowl very well until it's put back together, and if we don't do something soon, he'll be permanently lame."

"I'm on call. What if I get beeped?" I had visions of having to dash away with cat bits lying all over. "And he ate not long ago."

"It's quick, really. Getting him anesthetized will be the biggest part. Eating isn't really a problem, I think." With that, he grabbed a handful of paper towels and cleaned up the inside of the box. I hadn't really tuned into some of the noises coming out of the crate on the way over.

"Okay. I'm game." Carrying Harpo back to the surgery area at least let me feel useful, and there was Dante's nice butt for scenery again. I had time to notice the wide shoulders, too. "Need to coach me, though."

"You get to monitor breathing and heart rate for the anesthesia; tell me if either rate rises or drops, and you get to hand me things. You know all the names, right?" He grinned at me, his teeth flashing. "Sorry to make you watch, but at least it's not your own knee."

"Yeah, but it's my fault. Me and my big feet." I watched as he drew out medications in syringes and kept Harpo from backing up off the table when Dante aimed one of the syringes at the meat of his thigh.

"I'm going to knock him out first, just because he's hurting. You know the drill." He beckoned me to the sink to scrub up once Harpo went limp. He had to interrupt his scrubbing to park the sugar glider in a cage before he gowned up.

His hands were deft and sure as he clipped the site and swabbed the leg, waiting only a moment for drying before he incised the skin with the scalpel I'd handed him. Nothing on that tray was new to me, aside from the small pin that he used to stabilize the joint while he took quick stitches in the tendons. The drill looked a lot more like a home improvement store item than what I'd used on surgical rotations, but otherwise, no big surprises, and he kept up a running commentary from behind his surgical mask.

"Okay, going to close up now," he said after what might have been a short surgery but seemed to take hours. "He'll be sore for a while and he needs to stay inside for about six weeks while the ligaments heal, especially if he's a jumper, but he should be very nearly good as new." He wrapped the leg with a sterile dressing after flexing it to ninety degrees and then straightening it. "Better already." He'd given Harpo a few more injections during the surgery to keep him sedated, but not recently. I wondered how long it would take the cat to wake up, and when I could take him home.

"Now this big guy needs to come to and find his feet. I thought I'd just take him upstairs and park him in the living room; then I can keep an eye on him and pretend there's something left of a day off." Dante stripped off his gloves and flipped them in the biohazard trash. "Want to come?"

"Sure." My beeper remained quiet; I cast a stern thought at it to stay that way as I followed Dante, the sugar glider he'd retrieved from its cage, and a sedated Harpo up the stairs. The scenery was still nice. I could see grabbing a double handful of that.

The stairs opened up on a small living room with an attached kitchen on the other side of a bar. Copper pans hung from hooks, but the main items of décor seemed to be animate. At least three cats sprawled across the room and a wall of aquaria held what were probably creepie crawlies. Toddler pens marked off two areas; one held a small dog with a cone over its head and the other had an open crate with a towel on the bottom. A fluffy tail was visible, nothing else. Something downstairs had seemed odd; there had been the usual rack of cages, but there was no one in them, save for a sugar glider and that only briefly.

"Does everyone come upstairs to hang out with you?" I asked, as Dante settled Harpo on a cat bed on the floor.

"Pretty much. A couple of these guys live here, but I don't see why the others should stay in jail all weekend just because the families went out of town." He arranged another set of toddler pens around Harpo and set out some dishes and a box. "Sit." The sugar glider went into a large cage where she disappeared into a nest box.

The couch was pretty well catted, so I picked up a white one with a brown tail and spots in order to sit under it. The cat seemed content to settle on my lap, driving some curved spikes into my knee to demonstrate. "What about the black and white one in the waiting room?"

"She's not very well socialized to other animals, and she's had all the company she can stand for one day, so I put her in there to calm down. It's really not solitary confinement." Dante went into the kitchen and returned with cans of soda. "She'll be a great pet for someone." He handed me a can and sat down, close enough to make me think I had a chance, but far enough away that he wasn't making a move. Or maybe it was the cats on either side that made him sit there.

I started to take a swig of the soda but was arrested mid motion by Dante taking a sip of his. Those full sensuous lips against the can made my breath catch;

his lowered eyelids partially covered the deep brown eyes. I wanted to touch his eyelashes, feel their texture. Instead, I stroked the cat in my lap until his tail flipped in annoyance.

"So, busy on call?" he asked, settling back.

"Yeah, up all night with a labor and delivery, a few other things. Had to put some kid's elbow back, which was a lot easier than what you had to do just now." I managed a drink of soda at last. The cat regarded me and my social skills through slitted eyes.

"Funny, I had an L&D, too, only I got five kittens. Mama and babies are in there." He gestured to the pen with the crate. "Scottish Folds, rather valuable, but she's a nice cat. More important, I think, but the shows are big business."

"Scottish Fold? I don't know what that is," I confessed.

"A breed of cat with ears that fold over close to their heads. Like this." He turned slightly and reached to my lap cat, pushing one ear over. His own ears were small and close to his head, nearly close enough to whisper into. Or kiss. I made a small choked noise in spite of myself for the effort of doing neither. He turned to face me without backing away. "Too close to the black guy?" he challenged.

"Not close enough," I blurted. Now he could get mad, throw me out, and tell me to come back and get my cat later.

"Really?" He hadn't moved.

"Really." I was frozen in place.

"You're gay."

"Yeah."

I was waiting for it all to come apart, but I might be waiting a while, because he kissed me. He didn't bring his body any closer; he just moved his face enough to meet my lips. I didn't close my eyes, because I needed to see him; he didn't close his either, and the challenge didn't leave them. Still, he kissed me, lips parting gently though neither of us tried for tongue, me because I was scared I'd make him back off, he, because...

Because I was a stranger, because I was white, because I was an experiment, because... Oh hell, I didn't know and I wouldn't until he chose to tell me, but that would mean ending the kiss and I didn't want to do that. He brushed his lips against me again, making me respond both with my mouth and with my cock. It hardened and rose; the hunter in my lap grabbed at it, claws out.

"Ow!" I dumped the beast off and felt for damage. Dante pulled back, smiling but not laughing, though I finally had to shake my head and chuckle ruefully. "Does he chaperone you all the time?"

"He... doesn't have much to chaperone." He shoved another cat off the couch and sat close to me, his arm around my shoulders. "Shall I do any first aid?"

"Yes," I breathed, not daring to believe this was happening.

Once again our mouths met, my thin lips pressed against his soft full ones, and this time I did let my eyes flutter shut. I had to slide down a little to fit against him; we were nearly of a height, though he carried most of his five feet eleven in his torso and I'm more legs. He held me and slipped his hand down the front of my pants. I pulled the knot out of the drawstring to let him have better access and was rewarded with a strong hand gripping my cock.

"Better check," he teased, pushing my soft pants down enough to expose my cock. "So far, no major trauma." He began to stroke me; I had to hide my face in his neck. Dante smelled of warm man, antiseptic, and soap; breathing him in was making me dizzy. Wrapping my free arm around him let me feel the skin on the back of his neck, and then I ran my hand up to touch his short hair. Even the texture of his hair excited me; when he kissed me again with those open mouthed, yet almost chaste kisses, I had to moan out loud.

"Hurts that bad?" he breathed, and no, it just felt that good.

The kisses grew in intensity—tongue met tongue, lips met lips and he kept stroking my cock, though before I grew aroused enough to climax he took his hand away to run it up and down my body under my shirt. I'd been doing the same to him, and somehow I ended up kneeling between his knees.

"May I?" My hands were at his fly; I waited for the go ahead before unbuttoning him.

"Yeah," Dante said, running his hands through my short, sandy brown hair. He let me pull his jeans off and the underwear came with them, exposing his muscular thighs that I'd tried not to notice when he'd come in for treatment. I noticed them now, with both eyes and both hands, and then moved to his cock, thick, uncut, and so hard. I wanted him in my mouth, and yet I hesitated. I knew something important about him, but he didn't know the same about me, and telling him now would be meaningless; it was the sort of thing that needed to be talked over while dressed and limp.

So I ran my lips over the shaft, flicking and nibbling, playing him with a hand as I slipped the other behind him to grab one rounded muscular buttock. Not slipping his entire cock into my mouth was one of the tougher things I'd ever done, but until we'd had that conversation, this was going be the safest sex we'd ever have.

His hand on the back of my neck urged me on but didn't push me into more than I wanted to do, though his moaning was encouraging me on to more than was wise. When he pulled me up for a kiss, he interrupted the temptation to take the head into my mouth, and then he stripped my shirt off.

He pulled me off my knees, slipping my soft jersey pants down over my ass. Grateful for the gym time I'd been putting in, I knew that my butt would be almost as nice to grab as his was, something he was busy finding out for himself. The sob came out of my throat unbidden, muffled against his shoulder.

Straddling his thigh with one knee on the couch and the other foot on the floor put our cocks so close together. I leaned down to kiss him, thinking that our differing proportions made this work well, and then I quit thinking as he put his hand on my cock again.

His cock was right there, throbbing in my grip; we pumped each other as we played lips and tongues over one another's. He didn't cry out until the end, as he pulsed in my hand; my own yell followed swiftly as Dante stroked me into an orgasm that contracted everything in my body.

Once the shuddering was done, far too soon, I straightened my back and slid next to him. His thigh between my legs was something I'd be glad to have more of, but now I wanted to sit close. We'd started at the wrong end of this; we needed to talk.

First he needed to pull his shirt off: his scrubs had caught our semen. Pulling the front of his shirt out as he pulled it up kept his face dry; we chuckled just a little as he mopped our groins with the wadded up fabric. He dropped it on the floor, stretched out behind me on the couch, and pulled me down to lie against him.

"That," he murmured, his voice deep, "was unexpected."

"It wouldn't have been if you knew what I've been thinking since we met." I didn't like confessing unprofessional thoughts. "I was going to ask you out the other night, but I wasn't sure if you'd welcome it."

"I thought you might have had more to say." Dante put little kisses on the edge of my ear between words. "Though I also thought you weren't supposed to date patients."

"I'm not. I'll need to relinquish care." I rubbed his arm with the edge of my thumb. "That is, if you want to see me again." Socially. I should have said socially. Maybe if I banged my head on the wall I'd get all the right words out.

"Is someone else in the clinic okay, or do I need the records sent somewhere else altogether?"

He heard what I hadn't managed to say. He wouldn't have said it like that if he meant professionally. "Someone else in the clinic is fine, it's just that I can't be totally objective about you." I turned my head to find his lips again.

"Imagine you can't." He rubbed my belly in little circular moves and then followed the treasure trail south, brushing his fingertips across the base of my cock before resting his arm over my chest again. "Not sure how objective you're being about us, right now."

"Because of...?" I'd make him say it. His arm was dark across my middle, my own forearm a pale contrast next to it, my hand a ghostly presence on his biceps.

"Because you don't know me. I don't know you. The sex was fun, but what else is there for us?"

"Whatever we find and make, I guess." He was looking past the obvious better than I was, at least out loud. "But I do know some things about you. Important things."

"Oh?" Dante picked his head up from the arm of the couch, craning to see movement in Harpo's pen, then lay back down. "Like my HIV status?"

"Aside from that, yeah. Mine's negative, too, but I don't expect you to take my word on it; you can see the results or you can stick me for the lab yourself if you want to. But more than that." I didn't want to offend him, but I thought it was important. "But just because of what you do and how I met you, I knew a couple of important things from the start."

"Better tell me." His voice was neutral, though his eyes were wary.

"You're smart. You have to be, or you wouldn't be a vet."

"So?"

"So, I like that in a man. Means we could have a lot to talk about, or some lively arguments, at least." I wasn't explaining this very well. "Dante, I didn't make it into vet school; I have to respect someone who did."

"So human medicine was your second choice?"

"Yeah. I'm happy with it, but it wasn't what I'd always planned." Lots of things in my life weren't what was planned. "I like animals better than I like most people. They," I hesitated, "they don't judge."

"No, they don't," Dante agreed, his eyes focused somewhere or some when else than in the room. "Their owners do, though. Doesn't pay to forget that." He brought his gaze back to me.

I'd take that as a warning.

"So, brains are good. What else?"

"Well..." I trailed off, because I didn't want to offend him and this next was a minefield.

Movement from Harpo's pen attracted his notice; he got up and crossed to the little enclosure. Instead of stepping over, he opened it and knelt down to the cat. I sat up to watch, and the view was fine as his knees splayed out and his cheeks parted. He stroked Harpo, who moved uncertainly under his hand but didn't try to get up. "Hey, fella, you want your man?" He stroked some more. "So do I. Do you mind sharing a bit? Even if he can't get a coherent thought out?"

Okay, hadn't blown it yet. "And you're ambitious. This is your practice, you aren't much older than I am and you've built this up. That's impressive."

He turned to look at me over his shoulder; his smile was blinding. "And that means I'm not sucking up to Dr. Hoyer for the bucks?"

"That, too. Dr. Hoyer isn't sucking up to you, either. I'm sure you've met that as often as I have." One of my feet had to be firmly in my mouth now. "But it's the ambition that I admire; the other is just a relief. My last boyfriend... Well, it got ugly."

"And that's over?" He'd picked up Harpo and now he was coming back to the couch. My mouth went dry at the sight of naked gorgeous Dante carrying a cat, the view only slightly spoiled by a bandage on a hind leg.

"Long time ago, more than a year." I scooted over and lay back while Dante placed my groggy kitty on my belly. Harpo looked confused, but he relaxed as I rubbed his ears. Dante lay next to me on his side, on the outer edge of the couch this time. His warm brown body would keep Harpo from rolling off. We ran our hands over his soft striped fur, now and again running our hands over one another. Whether it was pain, confusion, or contentment that made the cat purr, he rumbled and vibrated against my middle.

"And one more thing..." I trailed off. "One really important thing." I could look up at his face as he propped up on one elbow. I wasn't going to tell him that he was the sexiest guy I'd met in a long time, that his tight body and crisp hair excited me, that I liked the very feel of his name in my mouth. Or at least not yet.

"Is getting information out of you always this hard?" Dante asked me with a lazy smile.

"Only at first," I admitted. "After a while you might beg me to shut up."

"I'll risk it. I know a way to shut you up." If it was by kissing me, as he did now, his full lips traveling softly over mine, I'd recite the phone book or read jokes out loud from emails. "But you have to tell me now— what's this important thing you know about me?"

Purring filled my silence as I wondered if he'd understand how important this really was. We stroked my furry buddy—would he get along with the other furry residents of this little studio?

"Dante," I said, just to hear it out loud, "you like cats."

On Call: Cat Clinic

DANTE WOKE me with kisses, his full dark lips finding mine with sweet precision. I rolled us over, his long warm body covering mine, skin to skin all the way down. We hadn't put anything on last night after hours of making love—we hadn't seen each other all week. I think he'd only slept enough to recharge; his cock lay stiff next to mine. A quick inventory to decide what to do made me pause, but he had already done that. Patting my legs apart, he rubbed a gooey handful of lube between my thighs, and another on my erection. I trapped his cock between my legs when he repositioned, and squeezed him tightly. I wanted to hold this man every way possible.

My own cock lay trapped between our bellies, the skin slipping against his stomach, rasped by the light coating of hair that decorated more than covered him. Every morning I woke up with Dante in my arms was a fresh day of wonder. I opened my mouth under his.

We thrust together, growing more frantic when he nibbled down my neck, settling in to work the big strap muscle on the side. I stretched to let him reach, and clasped his cock more firmly below. The direct circuit from neck to cock woke my orgasm—I clenched everything against the growing eruption, which shook me from head to toe, boiling through my groin. Dante held me through it, one strong hand on my ass, bucking harder when he was sure I'd finished. Maybe I held him too tightly—he collapsed against me once his own exquisite shudders had passed, leaving a warm stickiness that I was too sated to do anything about just yet.

"Mmm. How 'bout we clean that up, take another little snooze, and I'll make pancakes?" I offered, once he showed signs of functioning. I upped the offer with little fingerstrokes up and down his spine.

"Wish I could." He glanced at the bedside clock. "I have to get up. It's Shelter Clinic Day, Keith."

"It's Sunday, Dante." I nibbled the edge of his little flat ear. "And I'm not on call this weekend." Our social life had to accommodate my medical practice. His veterinary practice put the occasional spanner in the works, too.

"It's my *pro bono* day at the shelter. You can sleep in if you want." He peeled off of me, to the annoyance of my fat gray Harpo. No respecter of good sex, that one— he'd jumped up on the bed to flop on our legs before we'd finished the aftershocks.

I did want another hour of sack time but not alone, and not covered with cats, either. A small marmalade cat followed Harpo onto the bed, pussyfooting up to touch my nose with hers. Dante stroked her absently on his way to the bathroom.

"Uh, Dante?" I examined the little orange kitty. "This one isn't one of ours, is it?" We had an ever-changing cast of characters, some regulars like his Domino and my Harpo, who was sixteen pounds of love and opinions, and some clients, who came upstairs with us—Dante hated to "keep them in jail because their families went out of town." Dante also temporarily adopted kitties, usually before finding them homes with his clients. Waking up with a strange cat wasn't entirely out of my experience.

He poked his head back into the bedroom, a toothbrush paused in his mouth. "No, Bitsy is a boarder, she's going home tonight."

She buzzed in my hands, accepting the caresses, and when I put her down on the floor, she scampered over between Domino's feet, rolling to bat his legs. He squashed her down with a paw before toppling and swatting without claws. This happened frequently enough that we referred to it as "the floor show."

"She acts like she's home."

"Yeah, she does. Are you coming?" Dante dug jeans and a scrubs shirt out of a drawer. "You don't have to."

"Sure." We hadn't been dating so long that I wanted to let him out of my sight for a chunk of Sunday. Maybe in a few months, or if we moved in together, I'd have enough time with him that a few hours wouldn't gape like a wound.

Not that I understood quite what I'd do when we got there. Probably give rabies shots.

We pulled up at the shelter, a cinder block building visible from the west-bound highway. The office area we entered was sufficiently soundproofed that the barking was about ten percent of the sound that beat on us once we passed through to the animal area. Every cat in the place had to have had at least one nervous breakdown so far.

"The cat area is soundproofed!" Dante bellowed over the cacophony. "So is the surgery!" He led me into a restricted section, and the relative quiet let me breathe again.

"Hey, hey, Dr. Dante!" Volunteers in green shirt and staffers in blue greeted him like an old friend.

"This is my buddy, Keith." Dante introduced me around. "What do we have for him to do?"

On of the staffers grinned. "Chad called in, family emergency. Keith, you could take over for him."

"Okay, no problem. What do I do?" I could find the big muscle in the rear leg easily enough for vaccinations; I'd done it before when Dante was pressed for time.

"You get kitty-box patrol. I'll show you where the stuff is."

Just because I had years of experience and could also wield a pooper scooper quite adequately didn't mean that's what I wanted to do. Dante smiled though. "You don't want to be assisting in surgery today, anyway, Keith. I have a couple spays and, oh, eight neuters."

"You got that right." Brrr. No. I knew it was part of his work, a backbone of his practice and probably the one hope these animals had of finding homes, but that didn't mean I wanted to watch, or worse, help. Bring on the cat litter. I left him to scrub up and followed the staffer back through the din to the cat room.

It wasn't rocket science, of course. The bank of cages had twenty-three occupants in twenty- two of the twenty-four cages, and every last one had a dirty kitty pan. I set to work.

Okay, it wasn't what I usually did when it was a matter of volunteer work—I tended more toward the Peoples' Clinic days that needed medical help for the species I specialized in, but hey, this needed doing and I'd volunteered. So far, two hissers, one back-out-of-reacher, several that permitted me to stroke them, and one that not only accepted caresses but dove into my hand.

Don't rat me out—I stopped the latrine duty long enough to play with that one, a two year old blue cream (weird description on the tag—she looked gray and peach to me) female kitty with a shaven belly and dotted scars that meant Dante or a colleague had done a spaying recently. Damn, she was cute, playful, and loved my shoelaces. I hated to put her back in her cage, but there were so many yet to do.

"I'll take you out after I'm done with the others," I promised her, clicking the cage door shut. She stropped the bars, anxious for me to release her again.

People came through the cat room while I worked, meeting the kitties and starting the process of falling in love. I could hope both that my little blue cream friend would find a family and that she'd still be there to play with once my tasks were done. A few kitties left with people and a staffer, and two didn't come back. I wished them long happy lives and lots of lap time. Harpo had come to my life from a shelter much like this one and I wouldn't trade him for anything.

Done at last. I washed my hands in the utility sink, for the twenty-fourth time—handwashing is THE best preventative for spreading disease and don't let anyone tell you different—and spoke again to the blue cream cat. "Ready to play, kitty?" She draped herself over my neck and licked my ear with her sandpaper tongue. I brought her to one of the "interview rooms" where she proceeded to demonstrate her great skills in scratch post use, toy swatting, and lap sitting. Her purring method was on the loud side. I didn't want to put her back in the cage.

Dante found us there, dancing the feather on the stick over the floor for pounce training. "Having fun?"

"Yeah. Pawlina is a sweetie." I patted the feather on my lap; she jumped in and nipped the string on the toy.

"Oh, you've named her." Dante sat next to me on the bench. "That's bad."

"Bad? Oh. You mean, do I want to keep her?" I did. She purred so loud. Harpo would sound like a freight train with her. I could scritch one with each hand and get the most amazing noise.

"You're already keeping her in your head, Keith." Dante took the toy away from me and stroked her gently. She collapsed across my knees. "There's a million cats out there, and a lot of them will tug at your heart. So many of them are anything but the Cat Who Walks By Himself. A lot of them really like people, and you're going to meet one every time you walk in here. Are you going to want to bring somebody home every time, or am I going to have to leave you home on kitty clinic days?"

"Your viewpoint is skewed because you've spend your day castrating dogs and cats."

"I've spent my day preventing kittens and puppies that have no hope of finding homes. There's more animals than homes, but the ones I've neutered today have a chance. Keith, listen to me." He turned my face to his, giving me dark solemn eyes. "You can't bring

28

back every appealing animal you see. *I* don't keep every appealing animal I see, and a lot of them pass through my hands."

"I know. You sleep with me but you're a slut for cats." Fluffy, marmalade Bitsy wouldn't be there tonight. Would Pawlina?

"Keith, think. We have an established dominance hierarchy between Domino and Harpo, and the transients respect that. The ones that don't stay caged. The fighting is minimal—it's mostly floor show. Bring another permanent cat into that and we may never see peace again."

"But..." I couldn't promise to leave both cats at my place when I came to stay with him, and would *not* give up my nights in his bed. A chance met cat wasn't worth my relationship, however young, with Dante. Sweet, smart, sexy Dante, who made my heart vibrate harder than purrs. "I'll put her back in her cage."

"You don't have to."

"You just said..."

"I did. But Keith, I can see it in your face—you've fallen in love. I won't take that away from you." He put his arm over my shoulders and pulled me near enough to kiss first the side of my head, and once I'd gathered enough wits to turn my face to his, my mouth. "We'll bring her home and see if she can get along with everyone else. If she can't, we'll have to rethink."

"I think she'll do okay, and if not, we'll know." I wanted this kitty, but I understood exactly what he meant, and had to agree. We did have amazing stability with the pets, and I had hopes of combining our households one day. Dante was more important than any cat.

We rose to our feet and I pulled him tightly to me, finding his mouth and then his tongue. Homecoming would be all this and more. Dante was right—I had fallen in love. Twice.

Only once was with the cat.

On Call: Dancing

"Let's go dancing tonight, Keith."

I looked up in surprise at my new boyfriend. Dante hadn't shown any interest in nightlife in the six weeks we'd been seeing a lot of each other. He was throwing some things into a pan in the kitchen, letting me lounge on the couch to play with his sugar glider. The little animal was climbing my sleeve while I twisted around to put her upside down—she'd right herself almost faster than I could reposition my arm. It had seemed a good entertainment for the evening, at least until it was time to take Dante's clothes off.

"Dancing?" The thought filled me with fear. "Not one of my favorite things."

"We don't have to go all the time, but once won't hurt you." He flipped the contents of the pan with the spatula—the smell of sautéing peppers was wonderful. "You aren't on call tonight; I don't have any animals that need tending. We never go anywhere."

I sat up and the sugar glider raced off to see what was on top of the python's tank. Dante's apartment looked like furniture in a pet shop—his career as a veterinarian followed him home every night, which was a matter of climbing the stairs from his clinic. My big gray tabby, Harpo, hopped up into the vacated space, shaking the entire couch. That cat did the opposite of pussyfoot—at least he washed his face like a normal feline.

"We go to the gym, we go out to eat, we go to the movies," I reeled off. "Why dancing?"

"Those are all places where we're really alone, if you think about it." Something else hit the pan and sizzled. "And I like to dance."

This was not good news. If I distracted him, maybe he'd put dancing off to another night. Snuggling up behind him, rubbing my groin against his ass, nibbling his little flat ear, got me a full body rub. "I like this kind of dancing," I purred. "The prelude to the horizontal tango."

Twisting in my embrace, Dante put his arms over my shoulders, waving the spatula behind my head. "It's all a prelude to the horizontal tango," he murmured between kisses, "but the music is better at Shenanigans." The pan required his attention again, which was fine with me. I liked to press against his back.

"What if the white boy can't dance?" I rubbed my cheek against the black fuzz of his hair.

"Everybody can dance. Don't pull a stereotype on me." He sounded irritated and took it out on the peppers he stirred.

"I'm not," though I had, and thought I'd better switch tactics. "I'm a physiological marvel; they said so at med school. The only true and documented case of being born with two left feet."

Dante wasn't listening. "White boys can't dance. Blacks have rhythm and big cocks. Stereotypes. I thought we were doing without those, Keith—we both know you aren't a klutz and I don't have a giant cock."

"It sure felt big enough jammed into my ass last night," I suggested. His thick six inches felt damned good in my mouth, my ass, my hand...."Let's stay home and investigate." I'd bottom for the next two weeks if it kept me off the dance floor.

"We can investigate after." He turned to face me again, treating me to an appraising look from those deep brown eyes at close range. "Are you embarrassed to be seen out with me?"

"If I was, I wouldn't go to church with you." Diagnosing was a doctor's business and I'd just found a relationship killer that had to be treated, stat. "What do I wear to Shenanigans?"

That earned me a smile. "Those tight black jeans will work, and wear the black ankle boots."

"What about a shirt?"

"When you dance for me later, you'll do it topless, but for the club, you can wear one of my silk T-shirts. It'll fit like skin." He rubbed a hand up and down my back—I responded by grabbing his butt. We kissed, but some little part of me was distracted by the knowledge that after he'd watched me dance, it would be he who was embarrassed to be seen with me.

All through dinner, Dante was cheerful, making me glad to have buckled on something that clearly made him happy. Whatever misgivings I had about the sort of figure I'd cut at the club were a lot less important than pleasing him, and his good mood was infectious. We laughed over little things and exchanged hot glances, each one a promise for what would come later. Besides, it might be a very short evening at the club—I had visions of some other doctor hauling me off in an ambulance, planning to pump me full of anticonvulsant medication at the hospital because he mistook my dancing for seizures.

I did the dishes while Dante dressed, a good compromise because he came out looking like a vision in a pearl grey V-neck silk T that showed off his buff body. It clung to the ridges of his lats and didn't quite show every ripple in his abs, but it made me gulp. The tight black pants showcased his ass and muscular thighs, and he smelled wonderful.

"How many fights am I going to get into when the other guys start hitting on you?" I asked with my nose buried into the curve of his neck. "If the way you look doesn't draw a crowd, then the way you smell will bring the hordes. It's even better when you get sweaty."

He dug strong fingers into the tense muscles of my back. "Jealous?"

"Territorial."

"I'm pretty good at saying no." He bit my neck softly. "Except to you."

Only the knowledge that he really wanted to go to the club kept me from dragging him to the floor right then and there, but one deep tonguing was all I took before we headed out the door. Harpo stayed the night with Dante's cats when I came to stay with him—my cat gave me an ear flick on our way out, which I chose to interpret as "Have a good time."

"I'm covered in cat hair," Dante observed. His brown and white cat, Domino, had rubbed his shins in farewell. He brushed at his legs for most of the two miles back to my place, leaving traces of Domino in the passenger seat.

"I have a sticky roller; we'll get you defurred." That was the only downside to Harpo, too—there was always a cat hair on me somewhere.

Dante followed me into the apartment and lounged on the bed, watching me change clothes. "You clean up nice, too, you know," he said as I pulled on the tight jeans. "It might be me getting into fights over you."

"Yeah, right." I made a face at him and dove into the black silk T-shirt he'd brought along.

That brought a throaty chuckle. He stood up in order to help me tuck the tails in. I wanted him to pull them out again—his hands on my hips and his mouth on mine fueled my desire. "Look at yourself." He turned me toward the mirror and stood behind me, his dark face visible over my shoulder. "Better haircut, looks good." He trailed a hand over my cheek. "Getting a lot of loving: happy face. All that gym time shows, lots of definition here, and this nice tight shirt to show it off..." He ran his hands down my torso to my hips. "Don't you dare start sending signals like you might head to the back room with anyone, or there will be fights."

"Clinging like a barnacle to your hand won't send that sort of signal." That was another thing that concerned me: what kind of gaffe would I commit? I put my hands over his where they rested near my groin. "Hey, are you going to want to dance with anybody besides me?" I met his eyes in the mirror.

"Maybe an old friend or two." He turned to study my neck briefly before nipping it. "I won't leave you stranded—those vultures would pick you off before the song ended." He thought. "What about you?"

"Just you." I didn't even want to dance with Dante, but he wanted to dance, so I'd dance. Unless I distracted him first…"Let's take care of the cat hair." I caressed the side of his head before grabbing the sticky roller from the top drawer and rolling it over his slacks. Up and down his thighs, his lower legs, and I picked up enough fur to need to peel the top layer off. He turned to let me de-cat his butt, and then I turned him again, to roll over his groin. Teasing him with the roller made him hard, so I kept rolling over the hump forming at his crotch, wondering if he'd take the bait or stop me.

"We're going dancing, Keith," Dante rasped, pulling me back to my feet. "Get your boots on!" He slapped my butt to get me to the closet. It had been worth a try.

As we turned off the side street onto the main drag, Dante tried to reassure me. "If you think of dancing as really prolonged foreplay, you'll like it a lot better." Damn, he'd picked up on my reluctance. I thought I'd put on my happy face.

"I'm good with that." I was good with anything that put me back in bed with Dante.

Shenanigans was down in Glendale, that enclave of singles and nightlife in the southern end of town—it was a fair drive to get there, made more pleasant with Dante's hand on my knee. I drove my Acura, which seemed more appropriate for clubbing than Dante's small SUV filled with cages. We stopped at a truly ghastly intersection, with three streets meeting, one at an odd angle that merged into the main thoroughfare, and that's where it happened. The little Honda tried to make the light, the mid sized SUV had edged too far out, and someone else in a pickup didn't stop in time and rear ended it. The night filled with screeching tires, tearing metal, and breaking glass. The horn started before the other sounds died off, and it kept going.

I wrenched the Acura to the side of the street—Dante pulled his cell phone out. Half aware that he was calling 911, I eyeballed the traffic and tried to estimate which car to check first. The Honda had to have taken the brunt of it, so I'd go to it first, though what I could do for the occupants without equipment and supplies, other than clear airways and put pressure on wounds, I wasn't too certain. I got across the street without becoming a pedestrian casualty.

The driver of the Honda was slumped over the wheel, blood gushing from her nose. No air bag had deployed when she'd gotten broadsided, though she'd been pushed across two lanes of traffic. I felt for her pulse in her neck; it was thready and weak, but still there, making me wonder what was bleeding internally. She shouldn't be moved until her back and neck were stabilized, which I couldn't do for her, though the sirens that started up in the distance said that someone was coming who could.

"Miss, can you hear me?" I implored her, though she didn't respond. "Miss, stay with me, stay with us..." I kept talking, reaching through the broken window, trying to assess the degree of break in her nose, wondering if slivers of bone had pushed up into gray matter. She finally responded with a weak moan. "Stay with us, hang on, help is coming." Wow, four years of medical school and that was the best I could offer? I wanted another pulse, and that was when I discovered that more blood was coming from her forearm at a frightening rate—a fountain leaped from her with every heartbeat. Other than some fast food napkins of dubious cleanliness floating around the car I had nothing to stanch it with—except the shirt off my back. I had the black silk padded against the wound and was applying pressure before she bled out in front of me.

Dante came up behind me. "The paramedics are on their way. The guy in the pickup is walking around and talking, but the guy in the SUV needs you, Keith."

"Keep the pressure on here," I told him. We scooted around to let him get his hand on the pad. "And keep talking to her." He started his comforting spiel and I sprinted to the driver's side of the tank that had stoved in the little car.

This man was slumped back in the seat, blood pouring over an otherwise gray face, and he listed sideways. The airbag lay deflated in his lap, telling me some things about the injuries to expect. His face was clammy with sweat, making me worry that all his problems were not related to the accident.

"Sir! Can you talk?" I asked, running my hands over his shoulder. The bone moved under my hand.

"Elephant sitting on my chest," he wheezed, which meant that injuries from the airbag were the least of his worries. I wanted to get him flat, but until the paramedics got there, which was, oh good, NOW, I couldn't.

"Sir, move out of the way," a man in blue with a badge told me.

"He's having a heart attack," I told the medic, sliding out of his path to the SUV's door. "Chest pain, diaphoresis..." I rattled down the rest of my physical findings, "and a broken collarbone on the left side."

"Everyone's a doctor," he grumbled. Another medic inquired about movement in toes and fingers.

"I actually am." He'd probably run into a lot of amateur diagnosticians, so I wasn't going to snarl. "Dr. Keith Hoyer, I witnessed the accident. This man needs nitroglycerin sublingual."

They lifted the man out of the vehicle and set him on a back board. "You always go around half dressed, Dr. Hoyer?" The slight sneer on "Doctor" set my teeth on edge—I dug into my wallet for a business card.

"Only when my clothing substitutes for a gauze pad," I retorted. "The girl in the Honda had an arterial spurt going. Dr. James is putting pressure on it. This guy needs some nitroglycerin, now."

"Oh, really?" sneered the first medic, but his partner barked at him.

"Get the nitro, dumbass, and be glad you've got a doctor!"

I watched him slip a tiny tablet under the man's tongue before going back to secure the straps. My watch crawled along as I timed the response—they'd probably be well away before five minutes had passed and we'd know if he needed another. I scrawled the order and my cell phone number on the back of the card, which hopefully would keep the paramedics out of trouble for following an unknown's directives, and handed it to the more reasonable of the paramedics before turning to see what had become of the girl. "His color is better already."

"It is," the paramedic agreed, raising the stretcher to wheel the man to the ambulance. "Thanks for stopping." His partner gave me a dirty look, but hey, there is a hierarchy and my dirty look outranked his.

The young woman had been transferred onto a stretcher of her own. Dante was standing back from the other crew loading her into the ambulance. The cops were here. They'd blocked off the intersection while I wasn't paying attention and now were looking around for people to talk to. Safety in numbers, I thought as I joined Dante; it would be better to be together, since I was half naked and we were both spattered in blood.

"Tell us what happened here?" one of the uniforms asked. His tag said Ladzicka, and he proceeded to walk us through every detail we could recall of the accident while the tow trucks winched the vehicles out of the intersection. Traffic through here would be miserable for another fifteen minutes after the wreckage was cleared.

"So, you're a vet, Dr. James?" Officer Ladzicka took some notes. "Do you always treat humans?"

Neither of us liked the antagonism in that question. Dante answered, "I was more of a Good Samaritan here, Officer."

"He was working under my direction, Officer," I interrupted. "He did nothing to assist until I ordered it." This was a sticky issue; Good Samaritans could get away with a lot more than could professionals who crossed species lines. I'd trust Dante with my life, but he was suddenly trusting me with his license. "Think of him as a Samaritan who knows the language." I fixed the cop with my best "intimidate Nurse Ratchet" look.

"Gotcha," he said, recognizing an authority that didn't have to answer to sergeants, lieutenants, and district attorneys. "By the way, where's your shirt?"

As a comeback, it wasn't nearly as effective as he'd hoped, because Dante held up the messy black silk, drops of gore falling from the hem into the street. The officer looked at the shirt, at me, and at Dante, before clearing his throat and asking, "How do I reach you, gentlemen?" We handed over business cards.

"We'll need copies of the accident report," I told him. "For our records. And of course, we'll want to know how the victims are doing."

Officer Ladzicka agreed to fax the paperwork over when he was interrupted by the tow truck driver.

"Hey! There's a dog in here! I can't take this dog!" The driver stood at the open door to the SUV, staring in horror. "I think it's hurt!"

It would be odd if it wasn't, given the violence of the crash. The poor mutt had probably been an unguided missile, flying through the cabin until it hit the dashboard. Dante was there in a flash, running gentle hands over the dog's head, sides, and legs.

"I won't know exactly without x-rays, but I think there's a break in one leg, and could be internal injuries." He turned over his shoulder to me. "Keith, we need to get her back to the clinic."

"There's a blanket in the trunk."

We bundled up the dog under the officer's watchful eye and settled it in the back seat of the Acura. Dante handed over another card. "Officer, will you please make sure that man's family knows we've got the dog, and why?"

"I will. Thanks for dealing with it." He waved us off with a smile, making me wonder how much effort he'd have gone to if we hadn't intervened. The tow truck hauled the SUV away, green radiator fluid bleeding from beneath the crumpled bronze body, the last signs of what had destroyed the evening.

I drove swiftly back the way we'd come, listening to Dante crooning to the injured dog. I expected some growling and snapping when he reached to the animal, but perhaps it recognized help, because it let him sit in the back seat without protest at a stranger being too near. "We'll get you fixed up, girl," and variations of that floated up to me, making me wish for sirens and flashing lights to get back to the clinic faster. The half hour drive seemed forever to me, and probably longer for Dante, who could do little other than comfort until he had more resources. The poor dog probably thought her world had turned into hell.

Dante leaped out to unlock the door and prop it open before getting on the other end of the blanket. Together, we carried the dog in on the makeshift stretcher. It was a smallish animal, part Border Collie from the looks, and didn't protest being moved around.

"Stand on here with me," Dante marched sideways to the big floor scale he used for dogs. "I need to know how much she weighs." We did an awkward dance as we weighed the three of us, and then came back to weigh men and blanket after shifting the dog to the table. "Three milligrams per kilogram," Dante muttered, calculating what to inject the dog with before taking x-rays. "Scrub up—I'm going to need your hands here." As he'd predicted, one broken leg plus some cracked ribs. "Vital signs are good; I don't think we've got internal injuries on top of it, but probably a concussion or she'd be snapping."

Clad now in yellow surgical gowns and latex gloves, we looked nothing like the spiffy club-goers of earlier in the evening, but we had to focus on the project before us. Dante's concentration was intense as he exposed the musculature. I handed him things as requested so he could insert pins into the bone. "There you go, sweetheart." He snipped the last sutures free of the needle. "They'll give you wet food for a while. There has to be an upside somewhere, right?"

Nothing else required surgical stabilization, though the cracked ribs would need careful monitoring for a bit. With the last bit of bandage wrapped over the splint, Dante pulled off his gloves and smiled at me in the first acknowledgement of success. "I think she'll be okay."

"You do take being a Good Samaritan to new lengths," I said, brushing my lips over his.

"So do you, Keith. That was a new shirt." Dante didn't sound too upset.

"I didn't have anything else to use, sorry. I'll replace it." I hadn't put on a scrubs top under the yellow surgical gown, and his hands were warm through the thin fabric.

One arm was for me, the other Dante used to caress the still-anesthetized dog. "I'm worried about the girl. What do you think about back or neck injuries?"

"She had a side impact, so it's possible. Wonder what cut her up so bad?" I thought back to the blood shooting from her arm. "The window was tempered glass."

"I don't know, but at least she didn't bleed out on our watch. There was a lot of crap in the car; something could have been sharp enough to cut her." Dante shrugged. "How about the SUV guy?"

"He was having a heart attack, so going straight to the hospital was the best thing for him. The sooner treatment starts, the better the prognosis." I helped him pet the dog. "But I am really sorry our evening of dancing turned into more work."

"You couldn't have driven past that, Keith. We had to stop." I got both arms and a taste of his lips now. "There will be other nights out. Let's take Fi Doe upstairs for recovery."

Wondering how he knew the dog's name, I pulled off my surgical gown and followed him up the stairs. Dante settled the patient into an empty bed on the floor and set up the toddler gates around her. Harpo had curled up in that bed six weeks ago to recover from the anesthesia after Dante had rebuilt his joint and he'd regrown some fur on the surgical site—now he leaped lightly over the gate to sniff the newest occupant.

"You do good work." My big gray tabby bounced back out of the recovery pen. "He's jumping like nothing ever happened."

"This girl should do as well, if she isn't addled from the concussion." Dante brought a pan of water over.

I watched him kneel next to the dog, check color on the inside of its mouth, and then go to the sink to wash his hands again. "Do you think you'll get paid for the surgery?"

"It won't be the first *pro bono* work I've ever done if I don't." He came to join me on the couch. "But I probably will. You, on the other hand..."

"That was first aid." I shrugged it off.

"Not that." He grinned at me, eyes twinkling. "As an apprentice vet tech, you get the experience and that's about it." He pulled off his shoes, threw them in the corner, and wiggled his toes.

"I get to learn from the best," I said, laughing at the thought of submitting insurance claims for surgery on the dog. "Come here, Best, you can pay me with kisses." His mouth was soft and warm under mine, and I was ready to nestle down and pull him on top of me when I decided that the lights were really too bright. "Let me up for a second."

His eyes followed me as I went to the switch and turned the dimmer lower. My nude upper body had to be contrasting against the black jeans; I strutted for him, putting a little shoulder movement into my stride. It was only spoiled a little by tripping over Domino, but Dante's chuckle got turned into a rumbling noise of appreciation when I turned around. The situation would be further improved with some music, I decided. The bright screen of the MP3 player put a spotlight on my face and shoulders while I punched up a playlist. He'd been so eager to go dancing—I'd give him as much as I could of what he wanted in a situation that I could handle. No judgmental eyes would see how badly I moved, and I could control the music. Playlist accomplished, I put the player back on its dock and the first pulsing notes came out of the speakers. A quick scan for feline obstacles in my path, and then I strutted back to him, hips and shoulders rolling seductively.

Putting my hand out to him, palm up, I purred, "Dance with me."

His eyes widened enough for me to see white in the dimness for a second before he took my hand and rose from the couch. "You do take my breath away," Dante whispered, folding himself against me. The guitars throbbed—I pulled him close, hoping I could follow enough of his movements to qualify as dancing. He steered us with his hands flat against the small of my back, our bodies rippling a little against one another.

With my face against the side of his head, I murmured, "I think I see why you wanted to go. This is good."

"Oh, yeah," he whispered back. "Real good." His cock had already come up, right next to mine; we rubbed through our clothing with each shift of our feet and sway of our hips. "Take my breath away," rumbled softly with the music in my ear as he nuzzled me.

The song ended just after we'd made one slow circuit around the dim living room. More confident than I would have been at the club, I kissed him full on, having to bend a little to meet his lips. I still had the ankle boots on, which boosted me an unaccustomed inch taller than Dante. The bending excited me, and I imagined myself bending down to reach his lips when he lay on his back with his ankles locked behind me. I shivered and moaned, but there would be time to get to that. The next song started.

Oops. I'd forgotten that this song sped up to a tempo I wasn't prepared for. Trying my best to match the speed, I managed to step hard on Dante's stocking toes.

"Ouch." He gave me a mock-stern look, but he couldn't complain he hadn't been warned.

"Sorry." I dumped a cat off the couch to make enough room to sit and pull the boots off. "Now you know."

"Get back here." Dante put my hands on his shoulders and his on my hips, moving me. "Feel the beat," he said, smiling from the not-quite-close-enough-to-kiss range. "Like this." He added some back and forth steps, nothing fancy but still a challenge. My forehead creased with the concentration of making every body part go in some different direction. "Oh, Keith, you're treating this like hard work." He pulled me tightly against him. "Just hold still for a minute—we'll find the beat again." The kiss he gave me was a great way to reset my rhythm and maybe distract him, because it set my hips thrusting against his.

"Good, good," he murmured into my mouth. "That's the way, keep doing that." He stepped back a few inches and brought me two steps forward and two steps back. "That natural hip beat and a little feet, you're dancing."

I tried not to make it into a task again. Some of the lyrics slid by my mind—"We bragged of things we'd never done"—and while I wouldn't call this dancing, it wasn't standing frozen in embarrassment or stepping on his feet, either. The song slowed again, which let me come close enough for his silk shirt to slide over my skin. The music would speed up at the end of the verse and I'd be ready for it, this time, though my erect nipples against silk nearly distracted me. The last refrain trailed off—I pulled him against my chest, wondering if we'd have kissed this passionately had we been at Shenanigans. Probably someone would have tapped my shoulder and told me to find a room, or a circle would have formed around us to watch me tip his head sideways to better thrust my tongue into his willing mouth.

The lilting soprano coming through the speakers dragged me back to the music once again—Dante's wicked smile said that he knew how close I'd come to throwing him on the couch. One last brush of his body against mine before he twisted my hips with the music reminded me of his earlier words, "It's all a prelude to the horizontal tango," but I'd keep to my feet just a little longer. Just a little. Damned little. We had to stand farther apart now if we weren't going to touch at the groin, but where was the joy in that? Lyrics grazed my mind again—"I can feel you 'round me"—and I meant to make that a reality.

His arms around me kept me from tripping over random cats and the pen around his patient—he'd prevent me from going over backward. Dante steered and I followed, relaxing into the music enough that the sensuality of brushing against him overwhelmed my anxiety. Besides, it wasn't going to be me on my back. I had plans.

Another slow circuit around the living room brought us close to the bedroom door. "I think I need to take you to the back room now," I whispered. "Or we're going to end up on the floor."

"Let's not scandalize the other patrons," he murmured in return, and led me to his bed.

The music sounded clearly in the bedroom— undressing became nearly a striptease as I peeled the pearl gray silk over his head to the slow beat. Dante brushed his bare chest against mine, still dancing, before his hands stole between us to undo first his slacks and then my jeans. Our feet weren't moving, though our hips were. We dropped each other's britches, struggling a little with the slim-fitting clothing. Dante solved the problem of the tight pants he'd chosen for us by stepping out of his own and then sliding to his knees in front of me. The black jeans came down and my cock was in his mouth before they'd reached my ankles.

Maybe he kept the rhythm of the music and maybe he didn't—my mind shut down when he wrapped those full soft lips around my shaft. Dante grabbed my ass with demanding hands, rocking my hips to his rhythm and sucking me, and somehow it was all part of the dance. I closed my eyes and rubbed my palms against his short-shorn hair, loving the scratch against my hands and the wet heat against my cock.

One hand came between my legs to play with my balls—Dante found my sack endlessly entertaining—but it didn't stay there, probing instead toward my ass. I could have spread my legs to let him reach more easily, but once he found my hole, I might not have been able to lead this dance where I wanted it to go.

"Up, Dante," I said, even though it meant taking his mouth away from my cock. He came to his feet and thrust against me, his own erection upright and trapped between our bellies with mine. I savored the slight taste of myself on his tongue as I probed his mouth again, and one buttock in each hand mirrored what he was doing to me. With each squeeze and caress, I pulled his cheeks apart, just a bit, a prelude to my plans, and he responded with massaging circles against my buttocks.

Licking soft sweeps against his jaw and neck brought my mouth to his shoulder, where the ridge of muscle got special nibbles and sucking. He pulled away with a little cry—had I bitten too hard? He put his mouth against my neck to reply in kind. Our hips pulled apart a bit, letting our hard cocks swing against each other and giving me the room I needed to put a hand on his groin. Stopping briefly to roll his balls in my fingers, I then leaned down enough to cup my hand under his ass. With two fingers, I spread his cheeks and waited a few beats for Dante to feel the anticipation before I curled my middle finger up.

Teasing his hole with feather-light touches made him writhe—I wanted to touch him to readiness before we ever fell on the bed, because once we landed, I had only one goal. Tickling him and then slipping into him brought the moans that were the real music of my night, and I didn't have to say with words who'd be on top. Dante found my mouth with his again and accepted my tongue between his lips.

Enough—I leaned over and brought us crashing to the mattress, his beautiful dark body trapped under mine.

"I laid out what we'd need," he growled, bucking below me. "Fuck me, Keith."

He didn't have to tell me twice. Lube and condoms that were supposed to be on the table were not there, though—it wouldn't be the first time one of the cats had swatted everything to the floor. I eyeballed the wrapper for punctures before tearing it open. I knelt next to him so he could roll it over me, and the lube he spread heated rapidly between my flesh and his.

"Over." I flipped him to his belly and used my hands to admire his thighs from my vantage point between them. "Damn, but you look good enough to fuck." He smiled over his shoulder—turning his head made muscles ripple up and down his back. "Think I will."

Lying down on him put my cock between his cheeks and my chest against his back, something I savored for a moment before searching for my way in. The head of my cock pressed against his opening before he grunted and let me slip in. The warm heat of his passage enveloped my cock—the tightness held me still for a moment before I had to move, and then the only sound I wanted to hear was our bodies slapping together. I curled against him with my arms under his chest, pulling into him slowly, touching him from knees to shoulders, but then I needed to see him below me and pushed up over him, thrusting faster with my rising climax.

Dante cried out each time I pegged him, his cock rubbing against the bedspread with every smack of my hips against his round ass. The music was still playing, swallowing any words he might have spoken, though I could hear plainly what he meant with every moan. Pulling him to his knees let me reach around to his hard, thick cock. I draped over his back and pumped him in rhythm with my own movements. My fingertips barely met around his girth, though it didn't matter, I could feel him tighten and buck faster against me as his own orgasm gathered, squeezing my climax out and into him. Shudders wracked me, freezing my hand and hips as I pulsed into his ass—he reached underneath and helped me stroke him, not losing the pounding rhythm that brought him to a screaming orgasm.

We fell flat against the bed, which brought my lips near his neck. I tried to plant a tiny kiss there, but could only pant, maybe because all my available oxygen had gotten used up down below. I slowly became aware that the MP3 player had cycled around to the beginning of the playlist.

"You take my breath away," I puffed, completely losing the singer's pacing.

"You take mine, too," Dante mumbled, "partly because you're heavy. Roll over."

Right. I managed to extract myself from his ass and lie next to him, where I could look into his dark brown eyes with the curly lashes that I found so fascinating. I draped my arm over his back and craned closer for a quick kiss, which was followed by his soft smile. We lay so quietly for so long that one of the cats jumped up on the bed and plopped into the small space between our legs.

"I think we should go dancing more often," I said, just to stave off sleep. "That was fun."

"It was." Dante rolled to his back and held out his arms for me to scoot into his embrace. The aggrieved cat—Harpo—stomped around until he found another comfortable roost on our thighs. "But we don't have to go to the club unless you really want to."

"I thought that's what you wanted." I wished he'd said that earlier in the evening.

"It was." The pause grew rather long. "But I didn't want it for good reasons."

"Why would you want to go, if not for a good time out doing something fun with me?" I wasn't sleepy any more.

"I got a phone call today."

That sounded ominous. I lay quietly, waiting to hear the rest of the story. Dante stroked my arm absently.

"Remember I said I'd gotten crazy a while back?" I nodded. Dante had come into my office with a case of cat scratch fever and worries about his HIV status because of that craziness. I'd treated the cat scratch fever and set his mind at ease about the HIV. "He called. Said he'd be at the club tonight."

Maybe the craziness hadn't ended and it wasn't treatable. The gentle motion of his fingers on my arm had to stop, right now. I jerked my arm away and he didn't try to stroke my chest. "So you wanted to see him?"

Dante's chest rose and fell with the deep breath. "No. I wanted him to see me. With you. I'm sorry, Keith. I pushed you into something I knew you didn't want to do because....Because I wanted to show you off, I guess."

"Like you'd caught yourself a doctor?" I rolled over on my back, away from him. Was Dante one who'd date Dr. Toad just because of the credentials? I hadn't thought that of him. In fact, I'd thought exactly the opposite, because he had his own set of credentials, as impressive as mine.

"Being a doctor doesn't show until you open your mouth, Keith," he responded with annoyance, in sharp contrast to the sheepish tones he'd been using, and now used again. "It was more that I'd found someone good. Kind. Happy to be with me. Good-looking doesn't hurt. But I wanted...." He rolled to his side to look at me. "I wanted to prove to him that he was a fool, and all I did was prove that I'm a fool." Harpo objected to being moved again and marched up to flop into my armpit.

"How's that?" I glanced at him. "Most of the rest of that list doesn't show until I open my mouth, either."

"I know. And that's why I'm the fool. Because going to the club wouldn't have proved anything except you were willing to go to the club." He reached across Harpo to lay his hand on my chest, squashing a grumpy *mrrp* out of the cat. Dante took his hand back. Good cat. "It was the rest of the night when you showed off the good stuff, and I was there to see it, but I was the one who needed to see it." He stroked Harpo instead of me—Harpo twitched his ears back. "I had to face it, Keith—I was trying to prove something to a selfish man who'd hurt me, hell, endangered me, with a man who's trying to please me, who helps other people, a good man who...who hasn't gotten up and gotten dressed yet."

I turned that over in my mind while he waited silently to find out how badly he'd screwed us up. "Yet. You really pushed every last one of my buttons tonight."

P.D. Singer

"I know." His voice was nearly inaudible. Whatever else he was going to say got lost in the thumping and whining from the next room. "I have to check on the dog."

I followed him into the living room and watched him kneel next to the animal. She tried to rise to her feet, but couldn't quite manage it. Dante propped her up and guided her to the newspaper, then the water dish, before putting her back in the pet bed. He dealt with the papers without looking at me.

"I'll need to watch her until she falls back to sleep." Dante kept his eyes on her.

"I'll do it." Leaving seemed too extreme, though I might do it yet, and I didn't want to lie in his bed after finding out how I'd been manipulated and why. Sleep was out of the question now—might as well stay with the dog while I thought about what he'd said. He started to object, but I waved him off. "Go back to bed, Dante."

He left after turning the low lights even lower, and I sat on the floor near the injured dog. She rested her head on my lap and accepted the absent-minded stroking. Poor girl, she'd gotten hurt tonight because of people, yet she'd been patched up and would heal because of people. Small whimpers told me where not to stroke—the bruising would be with her for a while. Still, she hadn't stopped trusting.

Had I stopped trusting Dante? Should I? How much had I blindly trusted already? How badly had I misplaced that trust? The questions churned, but answers didn't come.

His words played over and over in my head. "Wanted to show you off." "Prove he was a fool." "Found someone good." "I was the fool." Eventually, another phrase he'd used floated up. "I'm sorry." I quit moving my hand on the dog and she quit scraping her front paws. Soft doggie breaths mixed with tiny scrabbling sounds from the sugar glider's habitat.

"So what do you think, Mandy?" I muttered to the little nocturnal creature. She clung to the wire mesh upside down and chittered softly. I filled in the words for her. "Maybe you're right." The dog didn't rouse when I slid out from under her snout, nor did the light in the fridge wake her. Mandy grabbed the slice of mango with two paws and tried to talk with her mouth full. "Okay, you're right."

There was enough light to see the liquid gleam of Dante's eyes on my way back to the bed. Slipping under the sheet with him, I turned him to spoon against my belly. Talking, no, I didn't want to talk any more—that would be for morning. For tonight, a small kiss at the back of his neck was enough. Harpo shook the bed when he leaped back onto it and plunked into the curve of Dante's body, followed by the softer tread of Domino pussyfooting to a comfortable spot in the crook of my knees. Dante's breathing went from ragged to even as he finally fell asleep against me.

We woke, festooned with more cats than we'd gone to sleep with, to the shrill of Dante's phone playing the business ringtone. Dante hit the speaker button.

"I'm sorry to call so early on a Saturday, Dr. James," said the weary voice on the other end. "My husband and dog were in the crash last night."

"How is your husband doing?" Dante asked, his voice crisp and professional. He rolled out of the bed to check on the dog. I followed him out to the living room where he ran a hand over her head and sides, still listening.

"He's going to be all right. I need to tell Doctor, uh, Hoyer, too, I suppose." The sentences were coming slowly. She had to have been up most of the night.

"I can pass the news along, if you like." The dog staggered to her feet and lapped from the water bowl. The splint on the front leg let her limp the few inches needed.

"Thank you." Long pause. "What happened to Mitzi?" I thought the dog's name was Fido.

"She had a broken leg and some cracked ribs. We patched her up already; she's up and moving, but she'll need to have wet food only for a few weeks." Dante lifted the dog's lip to check the color, healthy pink, as far as I could tell. "She's doing well. You could probably take her home in a day or two."

"Thank you. My son will come to get her, then."

After a bit of critter maintenance—kibbles, glop, walkies, and a gerbil that went from the gerbil tank to the ball python's, all accomplished in near silence—Dante and I sat on the couch to drink some coffee. It was one of those "made for conversation" moments, though he looked apprehensive over what he might hear. He probably wasn't expecting what I did say.

"So, are we going to dance again tonight?" I asked, playing my hand over the back of his neck.

"I thought you didn't want to go to the club." He set the cup down. The liquid splashed almost over the rim, though it was half empty.

"I didn't say that. Maybe in a few weeks, after you've coached me some more, we'll go to the club." I refreshed our cups. "But I liked dancing last night—I want to do it again."

"Okay." He looked puzzled, like I shouldn't be changing my mind from one day to the next. Or like he missed hearing the words that lay between the words. Or did hear them but didn't believe them. "Even if he might be there?"

"Even if. But when we do go, Dante James—" I leaned over to claim his mouth. "You don't dance with anybody but me."

On Call: Family

UNPLEASANT TWITTERS made me open one eye. Today was Sunday, and if it was still morning, it was too early. Dante and I may not have stayed up terribly late Saturday night, but we'd exhausted each other pretty thoroughly.

"I'm going to have to go to church with my family this week, Keith." Dante rolled over to slap the alarm clock silent. "My cousin's baby is getting christened. I need to be there."

"What do you want me to do? I'll stay home, if you want." After a couple of months together, we'd fallen into the habit of going to services at a gay-friendly church up in Boulder, an extremely liberal college town about twelve minutes up the road. Neither some hand holding nor the color contrast of the hands raised a single eyebrow there.

Dante's family lived about thirty minutes the other direction, in Denver. I'd met them for dinner, a rather tense affair, but polite. His parents weren't entirely reconciled to Dante's sexuality, and they sure weren't reconciled to me. We hadn't tested them further. His sisters Ellen and Shanya had been cordial, which was a relief.

"I'd like you to come. Keith, we're going to have to actually be seen together if they're going to accept us being together." He sat next to me on the side of the bed, running his hand through my short, light brown hair.

"Am I going to stick out like the proverbial sore thumb?" His family was one thing—his community another, and I didn't want to make trouble for him.

"Not really. Park Hill is a well-integrated neighborhood, and the congregation is, too. You won't be the lone paleface." He tugged me to sitting and wrapped his arms around me.

"Is that a politically correct term?" I had to twit him.

"No. You don't mention that I called you that and I won't mention how you got soppy and called me 'darling' last night."

I groaned. "So my brain disconnected from my mouth. Explosions in the groin will do that."

"They teach you that in medical school?" He laughed, rising and opening drawers for fresh clothing. Some socks came out and Harpo jumped in. Instead of chasing him out, Dante left the drawer open for my blobular cat, all sixteen pounds of him. The critters had the run of his apartment on the upper floor of the old house that contained his vet practice. Except, thank goodness, for the ball pythons and the tarantula, which stayed in their tanks.

"They taught me a lot of stuff." I got out of bed to cuddle him from behind, rubbing his belly very nearly the way I rubbed the cats'.

He turned in my arms to face me. "Best get into the shower—we have a longer drive than usual." I collected the one pair of brown socks and shut the drawer. Harpo must have tired of the unsteady footing among the balls of socks.

59

I got a little groping in while running the sticky roller over Dante before we left. His navy blue pinstripe suit collected evidence of cat ownership, as did my brown worsted wool. "If we wore nothing but gray, we could save some time on this task."

"Boring." Dante swiped the roller over me, making the contents of my pocket rattle. I'd left a prescription pad in there; no point in unloading just for church. He adjusted the knot on my salmon checked tie and brushed his lips across mine. "I'm glad you're coming."

We spent the drive down to the east edge of town with Dante filling me in a little more about where he'd grown up. "Park Hill is a stately old neighborhood; a lot of the houses date back to the twenties and still have enormous boilers for heating. There's some smaller fill-in houses and some scrape-offs that won't last much longer. The northern edge is rougher, always has been, as long as I can recall, but you don't hear so much about trouble there anymore." He glanced over to see my reaction to the reality of his life.

"Sounds like an interesting place." His stories weren't helping my yo-yo of emotions, though it was something different to concentrate on than whether or not his father would speak to me this time.

"It's a city neighborhood—a lot of stuff going on." He looked back at the road. Okay, I was a small town boy, where everyone knew everything about each other, good or bad, but that's because there were fewer of us. This was the same thing, I suppose, on a bigger canvas.

"Anyway, there'll be a collation after, where everyone will be salivating after one or the other of us, so brace yourself, unless you actually kiss me in front of everyone." He laughed. "If we were players, we could have different dates every night with the ladies of the congregation."

"I'm taken, thanks." I had to pat his knee.

"Me too—just saying."

Turning off the main thoroughfare at a corner with a large chain drugstore on the corner, we came upon a stately grey stone church of simple design; the huge elms shading it must have been saplings when the neighboring Art Deco houses were built. Clumps of people of every hue but all in Sunday best clothing swept toward the steps and open double doors, hailing each other and occasionally Dante. I received some speculative looks and handshakes before we reached the pew where Dante's mother was holding court.

Elegantly clad in a royal blue suit and a frothy confection of a hat, she graciously held out a hand to me. "How good to have you worship with us, Keith." Dante's father gave me a sideways look and a less effusive greeting. I sat, letting Dante buffer me from his parents. He chatted with them, only minimally engaging me, giving me the opportunity to look around. About half the ladies sported fanciful hats. This had to be the Basilica of St. Milliner the Divine. I kept that politically incorrect thought to myself. Dante had a way of making me rethink some of my less suave jokes.

The service started at last, not as unfamiliar as I had feared, though the choir, as integrated a group as the congregation, was the most in tune of any I had ever heard. Stand up, sit down, sing, be exhorted to good— all familiar. Dante's sonorous voice beside me led me through the needed responses.

Sneaking a sideways look at Dante and his parents, I caught their love and pride over their family's newest addition. Dante's cousin, whom I had not yet met, and her beaming husband brought their tiny baby forward for her introduction to the congregation, and that's when I saw Dante's father double over, his face ashen.

"Psst! Dante!" I elbowed his attention away from the font. His eyes widened, taking in his father's distress and mother's panic. "Let's get him out of here!" With one of us on each side, we managed to extract him from the pew and mobilize him down the outer edge of the sanctuary, Mrs. James following. "Where?" I hissed.

"The quiet room." Dante steered us to the soundproofed area, which mercifully contained no howling infants. We set Mr. James down, and I started my assessment.

"Chest," he was able to tell me. "No," when I asked about arm pain, history of kidney problems, "yes" for high blood pressure, which worried me. Still, the constellation of symptoms I was afraid I'd find was not there, and his pulse was only mildly elevated. His age worried me less than his genetic background, because African-Americans have some significant cardiovascular risks. I'd try something that would differentiate between what I thought he had and what I feared he had, before we called 911.

"Dante, how fast can you get to that drug store? If the pharmacy's open, have them fill this." I whipped out the prescription pad I'd carried along by accident and wrote a script. "Get some antacid, doesn't matter what kind, diphenhydramine liquid, and the lido if they'll fill it. Then we'll know."

It was a small eternity before Dante returned from the two block round trip, but Mr. James didn't deteriorate, giving me hope. His wife held his hand, giving me imploring looks to "Do something" while I kept count of his pulse, which stayed lower than bigger problems would bring it. "This is what they'd give you in the ER, sir." I folded a stray pledge card into a crude cup, poured a big slosh from each of the three bottles, and held it to his lips.

He drank, and the effect was apparent in a scant minute. "What was that, Keith?" Mr. James sat straight, his color returning, to all effects a new man. I suspected I was speaking to someone else—he'd called me by name, a first.

"We called it GI cocktail, and it's a quick differential test for heart attacks versus severe heartburn." I capped the bottles, marveling at the lack of label on the lidocaine. Had Dante threatened or sweet-talked the pharmacist? He was pretty persuasive. "Did you eat something recently that triggers heartburn for you?"

"Well... I had some of Ellen's chili from last night, just for a snack...."

"Dad, you ate Ellen's thermonuclear chili!" Dante was aghast. "I can't eat that without pain!"

"It's good though." Father and son exchanged sheepish looks that told me to lay in a couple of bottles of this and that for when they next ate Ellen's cooking. He turned to me. "Thank you, Keith. We aren't going to miss the entire service."

We had missed most of the christening, but unfortunately, we got the entire sermon, which the four of us listened to in the quiet room. "Love thy neighbor as thyself" was the text, but I thought we were all doing pretty well before the minister started talking.

Later, at the collation, Mrs. James watched with an eagle eye what her husband served himself, and introduced me to everyone who came near as "her son Dante's friend." Mr. James sidled back toward the buffet and some of the previously forbidden items landed on his plate. I surreptitiously transferred the bottle of antacid from my pocket to his, earning a wink. Dante and I made our exit, after duly admiring the baby who was the center of today's attention.

"You'll both be back next week?" Mr. James clasped Dante's shoulder; Mrs. James kissed my cheek.

Dante let me answer. "Yes, we will. Thank you." I shook Mr. James' hand, glad that his grip was strong and his bearing upright, delighted beyond words that his distress had been nothing worse than heartburn, and grateful, too, that he was willing to have me around. Dante had a firm place in my heart, and I didn't want to make him choose between me and his family.

"That could have been a lot worse." Dante aimed us back up the highway after the collation.

In so many ways. "I'm glad it wasn't."

"I'm glad you were there to take care of Dad." He pulled into the crushed stone driveway in front of his practice and home. I was beginning to feel that it was my home, too, although my cats and I travelled back and forth to my increasingly unused apartment.

"So am I."

"I think he likes you better now."

"A bit." I squeezed Dante's thigh, mindful that I had bought my acceptance with professional coin, but still pleased that his family's moment had not needed to be interrupted with sirens and paramedics that were in the end unnecessary.

We stripped off our suits and didn't bother putting anything else on, stopping to hold each other tightly and exchange some melting kisses. The skivvies might be coming off in a moment, once I'd nuzzled him again, or we might put on jeans and do some chores, but strange noises from the dresser distracted us before we made a decision.

The wooden chest shook, and weird howls emanated from its depths. Dante and I looked at each other, perplexed, and then at the possessed furniture. Gingerly, Dante pulled open a drawer.

Nothing happened, then the chest shook again. He shut it faster than he'd opened it.

Dante pulled open the next drawer, revealing nothing but socks. Again the shrieks resounded, louder now. Dante shut the sock drawer, and reached for the next set of knobs.

He had to really tug, because this drawer was loaded with shirts and sixteen pounds of angry tabby cat. Harpo leaped out and began to alternately berate us and lick his rumpled fur. With an aggrieved glare, he gave his side one last lick and marched from the room, *I meant to do that* radiating from him.

"He must have squeezed down one drawer and then I shut him in." Harpo really hadn't been in the socks when I closed that drawer.

"I have had enough surprises for one day. I'm going back to bed." Dante peeled down the gray athletic underwear that hugged his nice butt. "Come with me."

We snuggled up, ready to resume the sleep we'd interrupted for his family. I had one arm thrown over his chest and my nose squashed against his neck, and a couple of cats using us for hammocks, about as comfy as I've ever been. About halfway to slumber, I almost didn't hear Dante speak.

Just before he fell asleep, he mumbled, "Think your folks will like me?"

On Call: Wildlife

THE BELL at the clinic door bonged—but why now, when Dante and I were only seconds from escaping for the evening? Dante and I cowered in the surgery.

"Please, Dr. James has to fix him, he just has to!" The familiar breaking tones of a young boy pleading with the receptionist came only too clearly through the swinging door. This was becoming a ritual: Eugene Moore would show up with a big covered basket, bearing some wounded wild thing. Dante would either do some repairs to the poor creature or gently put it out of its misery. It had been nearly two weeks since the twelve-year old had turned up with a wounded fox for which we'd held a requiem.

Of course, he'd come in at five p.m. on a Friday afternoon. I'd gotten out of my own office at four, a small consolation for being on call this weekend. Right now, I wasn't sure who had the worse hours: a family practice physician, or a small animal vet, but I was leaning towards Dante just at the moment. It wasn't my receptionist who was being begged for aid by the pubescent Doctor Doolittle.

"He's back. I wonder what he's got this time," Dante whispered. Eugene turned up every time he feared his low-tech veterinary skills wouldn't save the patient.

"Could be anything with fleas," I muttered back. "Considering he collects them along a busy city street cloaked as a country lane." Dante's practice was in a house about two blocks off the main drag. The surgery was on the ground floor, Dante's home on the upper floor.

"Ain't that the truth. The construction on Kipling is forcing the traffic over here. Too bad the critters find out about it the hard way. Come on, Keith; let's go see what he's got." Dante gave me a clandestine kiss before heading to the door.

Arguing that the critter was uninsured would get me nowhere, nor would pleading dinner plans. It was part of Dante's charm that he'd help others when the need arose, although for some reason, need frequently arose around him. He could make the same claim about me. I shut up and followed, evening plans pushed to the back of my mind.

"Hey, Eugene, what do you have?" Dante took the basket, which was starting to shake. "It seems pretty lively."

Or mad, I thought. Maybe the mystery organism was small with blunt teeth.

"I don't know if it's a weasel or a ferret, but it's long and bendy. It just got hit by a car, and it bounced," the kid sniffed. "And then it lay still."

"It's not still now, Eugene. I don't think we should mess with it. It's a wild animal and it will be totally terrified if I touch it." Dante put his hand over the flaps of the basket to keep the inhabitant from escaping prematurely.

"Can you just look? Please? What do you think, Dr. Hoyer?" The kid turned serious eyes on me, slowing me up when what I wanted to say was "Let's let the damn predator go!"

What came out of my mouth was "Maybe if we get some halothane in there before we open the basket, it will be sedated enough to handle."

"Have fun, guys." Amanda, the receptionist and vet tech, had sworn "never again" to Eugene's projects after a bad encounter with a bat. She waved and headed out; it was after five.

Domino, one of Dante's resident cats who had the run of both upstairs and downstairs, sidled by, interested in the denizen of the basket. He rose and sniffed. The basket gave a good shake. A hiss escaped both parties and Domino was gone. Smart cat.

"Good thought." Dante led us through the swinging doors into the surgery, where he'd put me to work. Four years of med school had turned me into a half-assed vet tech, or so he'd informed me after I'd gotten dragged into yet another emergency procedure. I worked for kisses, I'd told him, so what kind of help can you get for that?

He set the basket down on the surgery table. "Keep the basket shut; we'll drip the anesthetic in through the crack." A layer of wicker didn't seem like nearly enough between my hand and an angry weasel; the shaking and hissing were growing exponentially.

Measuring out what would be an iffy dose of anesthesia under any circumstances, Dante returned in time to see our plans go up in shards of wicker—the hinge on one of the flaps gave way. A long skinny shape slipped out and ran.

It shot toward a rack of cages against the wall, creating total havoc among the creatures inside. Howling, mewling, and terrified yips greeted the wild invader. The situation wasn't improved by three humans floundering around madly, trying to get out of the way of the teeth. Perhaps it could have gotten under the cages, but noise convinced it safety lay elsewhere. Perhaps on the other side of Eugene, who wisely vaulted to the exam table. Dante evaded the wrong way, and if I wasn't making some really undignified noises of my own, I'd tease him about yelling when Angry Weasel made a brief trip up his trousers to about knee height.

The damned thing caromed around the room, looking for some kind of refuge, when Dante had the first really good idea in this entire debacle. He opened the sliding glass door, offering the creature a way out. I encouraged it with a broom hastily grabbed from a corner. Sweeping our unhappy guest in the right general direction gave it the message—the critter shot out into the back yard. Maybe it would keep going until it reached its den, or possibly Nebraska. Shutting the door on our unwilling patient, Dante heaved a sigh of relief.

"It must have just been stunned." He wiped the sweat off his forehead with a sleeve, though his dark features still had a slight shine. I loved that look; I'd have to kiss him all over the gleaming spots, once I was no longer pink from the exertion.

"Do I still have to cut the lawn tomorrow?" Eugene asked, hopping off the table. A twelve-year-old's budget and hefty vet bills brought him into frequent contact with Dante's lawnmower.

"After that, I think you'd better edge, weed, and get the neighbor's yard, too." Dante was still breathing hard and a small pulse jumped in his throat. At Eugene's crestfallen expression, he softened. "Just mow."

"Okay." He must have thought Dante really meant all that extra work, because he brightened way up. Dante's next words dimmed him again.

"Also, any more small potentially violent creatures have to arrive in a proper cage, for everyone's safety. Remember the bat?" We all recalled the bat—we'd had to extract Amanda from under the desk once we'd captured Little Dracula. There had been promises of a cage then. "Or I can't treat your critters, and you shouldn't be handling them unsafely, anyhow. You've got a big heart, kiddo, but you have to be sensible about this. You understand?"

Eugene nodded. "I'll get a cage, and I'll come mow tomorrow about nine." He grabbed the basket, which whiffed unpleasantly of the weasel and was now useless for picnics. "Thanks for trying, Dr. James." He showed himself out.

One the door clicked shut behind him, Dante came for a hug. "That kid's charity cases are going to be the ruin of me."

Literally, I thought, mulling the image of the weasel running up his leg, and the laughter grew until it couldn't be stifled any more. What came out sounded like "Snork!" and in spite of my resolve and knowledge, it just kept going until Dante was laughing with me. "You do a terrific Weasel Dance," I finally choked out.

"With the right props, so could you. You get the next weasel," he warned me. Unfortunately, with Eugene around, there would be a "next weasel."

"Imagine all those teeth heading toward your junk, and you'd scream too."

"Hey, I scream when it's your hands on my junk." I kissed him and rubbed across his body. "I scream when it's your mouth on my junk. I do a lot of screaming when I'm around you, come to think of it." Our cocks were growing as we crushed together.

"You're going to be around me, all right, and all your screams are going to be from pleasure." Dante nipped at my mouth and then smacked my ass. "Get upstairs!"

I ran, not so fast that he couldn't get a few more swats landed, but fast enough that he had to work at it. He chased me upstairs, across the tiny living room, and into the bedroom. A quick scan for cats before I leaped to the bed let me miss Harpo and Domino, though they bounced off the mattress and came down running. Dante pounced on me, wrestling my shirt out of my trousers and nipping softly across my belly with those full, soft lips I loved so much. Then he bent to gnaw at the fabric covering my erection before undoing my britches and hauling them down.

My cock jumped free of the fabric to be grabbed, the skin pale against the deep umber of his hand, shading to pink. Waiting for the delicious feeling of sliding into his lips, I closed my eyes, only to open them with a bit of alarm at the clicking sound. Wickedly, he gnashed his teeth again.

"I'm sorry! I shouldn't have teased you about the Weasel Dance!" Sitting up and grabbing his head before rationality returned at least let me feel his short cropped hair, crisp against my palms. He wouldn't really bite, I knew, but it made me appreciate his feelings about the weasel a bit better.

"Damned right!" Then my cock was in his mouth and neither of us had a coherent word to say for quite a while.

With a last nibble on my inner thigh, he lifted his head, hunting on the bedside table. "Lube?" He ignored the baby oil we'd rubbed each other down with the night before. "Ah." A couple of items landed on the bed next to me as he stood up and dropped trou.

I could look at him forever, standing over me with his cock so hard and proud. Shame to cover it up with a condom, but I did, adding a generous dollop of slickness. He kissed me as I rolled the latex down, his hands on my shoulders, and then pushed me flat again and flipped my legs up.

"You gonna scream here, Keith?" he asked, as he pushed into my ass.

"In a minute, yeah," I gasped as he breached my ring and filled me with hard cock. Torn between wanting to look and wanting to only feel, I finally closed my eyes as he withdrew nearly to the tip, then eased back in. Oh yeah, I'd start screaming any time now, and he worked back in to get the sounds he wanted. Pegging my gland every few strokes and then consistently wrung the noise out of me, and his strong hand around my cock turned the volume way up as I came, pulsing and spurting onto my chest. More shouts of pleasure erupted from Dante soon after, and he collapsed onto the bed at my side. Our dress shirts were rucked up around us, and damp spots speckled mine. Throwing an arm over him hid the mess.

"Guess we need to change before we go out, or do you just want to order some Chinese food?" he mumbled after we'd settled into the warm post-coital glow. We'd originally thought to hit a club, but we'd already done some dancing tonight.

"Let's order in. Lemon chicken, Mongolian beef, and make sure they throw in one of those place mats," I suggested, trying to keep a straight face as I stroked his back under the dress shirt.

"We need that why?" He played with my ass cheek, rolling it under his fingers.

Should have thought about where his hands were before I answered. He he pinched me hard for suggesting, "So we know when it's the Year of the Weasel."

On Call: Dante's Wish

KEITH HADN'T moved in front of the mirror for several minutes, not because he was vain. He wasn't even looking at himself; he was holding the ends of his tie, but his head was bowed and his eyes closed. Dante shrugged into the charcoal gray suit coat and came to help his lover.

"Let me get that," Dante told him, and took the silk from his unresisting hands. "Chin up," he almost said, but stopped, not wanting the request to sound like a demand for a changed attitude. Keith was grieving, and if he hadn't said why, Dante could guess some of it. With a gentle finger, Dante tipped Keith's head enough to tie a four-in-hand at his throat.

"I'll drive."

Their destination was a small church a few miles distant, a ceremony for a young man whose name Dante had never heard before, but who clearly meant something to Keith. He'd explain when he was ready, Dante knew; sooner or later Keith would be willing to talk. What little he'd said—"A patient"— was a clue to why he was so torn up.

Dante pulled his small SUV, the back equipped with the animal cages he needed professionally, into the church parking lot, careful to avoid the streams of people, many of them young, all of them solemn. He glanced up at the steeple and kept his wish to himself: he wanted to drive to a church with Keith, with smiles and flowers pinned to their lapels, to make some binding promises in front of people who'd shed happy tears. That wasn't going to happen today, or maybe any day ever. Dante dragged his head out of the clouds and turned to Keith.

"We're here."

Keith nodded without looking up, but didn't reach for the door handle. Reaching across the console, Dante took on of Keith's hands, lying slackly in his lap, and squeezed. "I'm here for you."

Keith squeezed back. "I know you are." That brought the corners of his mouth up just a smidge, for a fleeting moment. Dante squeezed again. "Keith, I will always be here for you."

Binding promises didn't have to be made inside the church.

On Call: Crossroads

My lover, Dante, sat next to me in the pew, holding my hand so tightly it hurt. The pain anchored me; it was the only thing keeping me from weeping openly. A tear slid down my cheek now and then as it was.

Today we were burying one of my patients.

I knew what killed him. I'd tried to prevent it. There was nothing surgical to be done, and damned little that was pharmacological, either, although an antidepressant might have gotten him through the worst of it. What would have saved him involved treating his parents as well, perhaps his extended family. Attitude adjustments, chiropractic for the soul.

Because I didn't think there was anything accidental about his little Ford meeting a bridge abutment.

Sixteen years old, male, well developed, no present complaints. John Samuel Carstens sat on the edge of the exam table, waiting to get stabbed with the tetanus vaccine that was the prerequisite for the summer camp where he was to be a junior counselor. John was in good shape from running track and playing basketball for his high school, and so far he'd given me no reason to think he was anything but healthy.

"Anything you'd like to discuss?" I listened for the er-ing and um-ing that meant something important would come out in a moment. "Girls?" An assumption, but a good default for his age bracket. I'd tried saying, "Boys?" as well a few times in the past and met stone walls.

"Mm, no. Got them figured out as much as I need to."

So did I. Keep them as friends, treat them like people, and call bullshit as needed. I wondered what his method was, and if it matched mine, and for the same reasons. I waited.

"Dr. Hoyer—what if, what if...girls aren't who I think about when..." He couldn't bring himself to use the words, but the little pantomime over his lap was eloquent.

"When you masturbate?" I spoke calmly and matter-of-factly.

"Yeah." His agreement was barely audible.

"First off, masturbating is natural and normal, especially for guys your age." I sat down on the little rolling stool, figuring that he could see how sincere I was if I was low enough to be in his field of vision. "It's nearly universal."

"It's a sin," he whispered. I stifled a groan. That one comment said that the 'not girls' part was going to be harder than usual for him to accept.

"It's a way of getting happy and feeling good that doesn't bring other people into it before they, and you, are ready for that." Once again I mentally cursed Onan, his legal dispute over his brother's widow, and

every Bible-thumper who forgot what the real problem was. It wasn't what he did, it was why he did it. Not an issue that I could really debate with the young man on the table.

"You really think that?"

"I really do. It's your body and a private matter."
I wished someone had said that to me about twenty years ago.

His face changed as he thought that one over, brightening a bit and then collapsing again. "But thinking about... while I.... That's wrong."

"A lot of men do. It isn't necessarily an easy thing to accept about yourself, but it isn't rare, either." This kid needed a lot more help than I could provide in the course of a camp physical. "Or wrong."

A tap at the door signaled my nurse with a tray and a syringe. Normally she would stay and do the inoculation, leaving me free to see the next patient, but I took the tray and shut the door.

"My parents are never going to understand. They'll hate me. They think every gay is a promiscuous 'ho' who's going to get AIDS and die a gruesome death and then go straight to Hell. Or should."

I stuck his deltoid with the needle, as much to get his attention as to administer the tetanus shot. "They're still your parents; they may have more flexibility than you think. Look, is there any way you can get some counseling? Think we can get your folks to agree that you need to talk to someone, without being specific about why?"

"They'd send me to the pastor, and I know what he'd say." No flicker of hope existed in that statement. "I'm already damned." I couldn't tell if he was predicting the

pastor's reaction or assessing himself, so despairing were his words.

"No, you're not." I guess I was going to have to argue theology with the kid. "Do you do yard work?"

That got his attention. "Yeah, why?"

"Then when you get back from camp, you can come over to the vet clinic at 92nd and Wickham and mow the lawn. That gives you a legitimate reason to be there, something you can explain to your parents, and we'll have some iced tea and talk afterwards. You shouldn't have to bear this alone. Okay?"

"I'll... think about it."

"I'll see you after camp." I'd probably broken every rule about separation of professional and private life, but this kid needed an outside voice in the worst way. He'd already opened up to me and found me non-judgmental; maybe I could help him find what he needed to get to a place where he wasn't condemning himself. And it wouldn't hurt one bit for him to see a committed, monogamous gay couple living a recognizably suburban life.

But I hadn't seen John again, not as a patient, not as a friend. Not even as a corpse, because his coffin was closed and would stay that way. The wreck had been brutal.

The pastor spoke of a young life cut tragically short by accident, and I wondered if he was the one John mentioned. We sang, or stumbled through, the final hymn, and then shuffled from the sanctuary of the little church. Dante's was one of the few dark faces in the small sea of people, which contained a lot of teenagers, all solemn or weeping. I was glad that his friends cared enough to be here for John, for his family.

"Are we going to the interment?" Dante asked softly. I shook my head "no." They were burying John in hallowed ground, for which I was grateful, but I couldn't bear to watch them do it.

"Let's go home."

Dante drove us back to the converted house with the "Cat Care, Dante James, DVM" sign in front of the first floor clinic and the second story apartment where we lived. The ride was silent; he didn't push me to talk, and I hadn't given him much detail beforehand. It wasn't the first funeral for a patient that I'd attended, but it was the first that I'd asked him to come with me. He knew that eventually I'd talk, but he let me come to it in my own time.

With a door between me and the rest of the world, I could yell my mind. "It's such a damned waste!"

I wanted to kick something, break something, hurt someone, preferably someone who'd convinced a malleable kid that he was insufficient and unworthy for being what he was, but the only one there was Dante, whom I wouldn't hurt for the world. The coffee table took the blow with only a creak, and I paced the small living room. "They say despair is a sin, but I say that the people who drive someone to despair sin worse. I had maybe five minutes to undo a lifetime of damage and it wasn't enough!" The leg on the coffee table collapsed this time, and I was vaguely aware that later I'd be sorry and have to fix it, but right now I just kicked it again and whirled away while all the books slid to the floor. Dante stayed to one side and listened.

"I did what I could there in the office, and I thought, I thought..." The words stuck in my throat; I tipped my head backward and tried to swallow the lump down. "I thought if I could talk with him more, if he could see..." The lump grew too huge to speak around —I waved a hand at our home, at Dante, at myself. "If he could see that being gay wasn't the awful thing he'd always been told, if he could see that a good life is possible..." I stopped pacing and stood, chest heaving. "But it wasn't enough, I wasn't enough, I didn't do it right..."

I would have kicked the coffee table again but Dante was in the way. "Keith, if you couldn't do it in five minutes, I don't think anyone could have."

"But I was the one there! I was the one who had the opportunity!" I flung myself across the room again, too tense to stand still. "And he still felt that awful." My voice dropped. "At least they don't bury them at crossroads any more."

Dante puzzled out the sense of it. "You think he killed himself?"

"Almost positive. Or courted death, telling himself he was only taking risks. But, yeah, Dante, I talked to him, and I think so." Clenching and unclenching my fists, I tried not to stomp around, because my fat cat Harpo had come to strop on my legs, despite the shouting. He wasn't intimidated by much, even me. Kicking him across the room by accident was a distinct possibility, but I couldn't stay completely still.

Dante noticed. "I'm sorry; that's really horrible. Keith, you're about to jump out of your skin. Go get your running shoes; I'm going to tire you out." He sent me to the bedroom with a slap on my butt, and came to get his own shorts and T-shirt.

Running wasn't something I really wanted to do, but the wisdom of his words got through. I had too much nervous energy to stay indoors, so I let him chase me outside.

We swung down the street, heading to one of the many bike paths that crisscrossed the city, and turned west toward the reservoir. Normally I enjoyed the route; the concrete would turn to unpaved path there, and we'd run through what was actually a nature preserve within the city limits. We followed the path under the busy main street and past a school at a pace faster than I would have chosen, making it harder to talk. I tried anyway.

"I should have—"

"Run faster." Dante elbowed me and sped up, reaching the dirt path ahead of me. Not fair, he could run considerably faster than I could, although I could keep going several miles farther if I picked the pace. Focused on my internal landscape, I barely registered the change in surface, except to wonder if John had been a runner, if he had used his athletic ability to channel his thoughts away from more uncomfortable feelings. Staying on the path was the extent of my outside awareness, and not turning an ankle on the loose stones.

We got past the prairie dog town, getting barked and chattered at as terrible dangers to prairie dogs everywhere, when I tried again. "I really screwed up. I'm not using my—"

"Run faster!" Dante commanded, pushing us to a pace that was my maximum, though not his.

At the water's edge, I stopped. "Making me run faster keeps me from talking but not from thinking, Dante."

He wiped his forehead with the hem of his shirt. "You need to really think, Keith. Not grieve out loud.

What could you have done differently? You reached out, you tried to offer help, you had one brief visit to talk to him, so what could you have done differently that would have avoided this?"

"I don't know." I barked back. "I just don't know. Maybe I need to go back to school, learn some counseling, maybe I need to practice somewhere that just keeping them from dying of sepsis from a small cut is considered good care, maybe— I don't know." I picked up a rock from the shore and hurled it into the water, startling a Canadian goose that swam nearby with her brood. "But I feel like a failure doing what I'm doing here!" I hurled another rock and the goose ushered her little family in the opposite direction. Good move, goose. "I feel like I need to expiate this, maybe go do some medical missionary work, I don't know."

"If you're going to leave for Haiti or the Philippines or somewhere like that, you need to give me enough time to sell the practice and brush up on diseases of goats."

I whipped around, jolted out of my rant by how serious he sounded. He gazed at me calmly, to all appearances utterly sincere about what he'd just said. "Diseases of goats?" I repeated, sounding stupid to my own ears.

"Yes, they're economically important animals in most places you'd go as a medical missionary. Cats, not so much; they reproduce pretty fast." He shrugged.

"Sell the practice?" I felt like I'd been slapped upside the head.

"Did you think you were going without me?" Dante did not smile when he asked that.

"No..."

"Then whatever you need to do, we need to plan together. Okay?" I nodded, and that got the first hint of a smile. "'Whither thou goest, I go.' For now, we run."

We ran.

I was exhausted mentally and physically when we returned, enough that my mind pretty much shut down. The wounded coffee table drew me—I knelt to examine the damage I'd done. It might not be fixable; I stacked the fallen books and tried to make the leg hold the table level. It wouldn't stay up.

The tears came then, blinding me, so I didn't see Dante come close, only felt his strong arms drawing me to my feet and embracing me. Against the firmament that was my beloved, I dashed my despair and grief, and he held me until the storm abated.

"Oh, Keith. I am so sorry." He rocked me gently from side to side, and I wept, for John, for his parents, who might never understand what they'd cost themselves or why, and for myself, for not being able to head off this tragedy. I'd replayed our appointment over and over in my head, wondering where I could have put better words, and what they might have been.

I lifted my head from his shoulder, the worst of the storm finished, though the ache in my heart would be there a long, long time. Dante's cheeks were wet. I thumbed one dry and licked the tear track away on the other side. In spite of my own disgustingly drippy state, he kissed me. "I know you tried."

"For all the good it did."

Another tear slid down his face. "At least you were there for him that little bit."

I knew his family had had a bad time initially with Dante's coming out. Even now, years later, his parents weren't exactly reconciled to it, although they'd been more accepting of me since the thermonuclear chili heartburn incident at church. Dante's father hadn't had a heart attack after all, something I'd been able to differentiate without hauling him to the hospital. "Was no one there for you?"

He shook his head. "No, I pretty much had to cope alone."

"How'd you manage?" *Did you ever think of killing yourself? I did.*

"I studied all the time. All the time. Best possible excuse for no social life and it paid off by getting me into vet school. And it kept me from thinking about things too hard." He grabbed a handful of tissues out of the box on the breakfast bar that divided the little living room from the kitchen, handing most to me and keeping one. "Except when it didn't." He shook his head sadly. "Growing up black, gay, and middle-class has got to be a lot easier than growing up black, gay, and ghetto, and no one accused me of being a sell-out for studying."

"Does anyone accuse you of being a sell-out for being with me?" I'd come close to pushing opinions on interracial couples back down certain throats with force.

"No one that matters." He put his arms back around my shoulders. "I grew up and quit listening to what 'they' say." He brushed my light brown hair out of my face. "I love you—that's the only important thing."

"I love you, too." I held him tightly. "John should have had his chance at this."

"He should have." Dante settled me on the couch against his body, my head on his shoulder. "There'll be someone else you can help, Keith." We sat quietly, long enough that the cats nested in our laps. A few more tears leaked out to stain Dante's sweaty T-shirt. I fell asleep to the sound of his heartbeat.

Peg feet marching on my groin followed by the thud of Harpo hitting the floor woke me. Dante's eyes were open slightly; either he'd been wakened as well or he'd been content to hold me all this time. He rubbed his cheek against my hair; I left mine pressed against his chest, feeling it rise and fall with his breathing. The room had gone dark with the passage of the sun and the air conditioner hummed in the background. Soft chittering from a cage by the wall showed Mandy the sugar-glider was awake; one of the cats meowed from the kitchen. All the sounds meant home to me, and love.

"How long do you think we'll be together?" I murmured, not wanting to move.

"Forever, if you want." He kissed the top of my head—it was all he could reach unless I sat up. "Will that work for you?"

"Forever sounds really good." I reached up to stroke his cheek. "Forever, us only?"

"Us only." His full, soft lips found my fingers. "It's been us only, it stays us only."

"I'd marry you if Colorado allowed it, Dante." Forever would have to be on terms we invented for ourselves. It's what we'd been doing so far.

"I'd say yes." He nibbled my fingertips some more.

"Think you can hit a human vein?"

That got a soft snort. He brought my hand to the cat in his lap. "I can get blood out of that, so I think so." Domino's jugular pulsed under my fingertips. I wasn't so sure I could get blood out of that vein; it was

87

pediatric size and I didn't do that many blood draws these days. "Why?"

"Why are we still using condoms?" We hadn't abandoned the safe sex habit completely, at his insistence.

"Because one of us has been waiting for the other one to say 'forever?'" He scratched under the cat's ear.

"We just said it. Let's go get some blood." I jumped up and pulled him to his feet. The cat leaped away, letting me have a full body hug. "Then dinner, then bed, where I'll show you what you have to look forward to for the rest of your life." I had to hold on to him; just saying all that pulled the blood from my brain, making me giddy. Dante, mine forever.

The drive to my office was as silent as the drive back from the funeral, though in a different way. We kept casting shy glances at one another, full of "what if's." What if one of us came up positive this time? What if we couldn't make it work forever? What if something happened to one of us? I didn't want to say any of that out loud, not here, not now, but my heart was in my throat. I'd only lived with someone once before and it had been disastrous. Dante had his own set of relationship traumas. The last had been just over a year ago, and it might have left the sort of aftereffect that would keep us in latex forever. It had brought him to my office and my life, sick with cat scratch fever, not quite six months ago.

I unlocked the dark office and turned on only enough lights to get us to the treatment room. I pulled two phlebotomy kits out. Before I could ask who got first stick, Dante held his arm out, his dark eyes calm and trusting. A hint of worry played around his mouth, and I thought again of his self-described "wildness" before we'd met. Drunk and bareback with someone who wasn't sufficiently trustworthy left him sweating out a seroconversion that fortunately hadn't happened yet and might never happen. We weren't still using condoms waiting for a declaration. We were using them because Dante insisted that he wouldn't do to me what his unlamented lover had done to him. I figured I'd fight it when the time was right. Like now.

"Are you sure you don't want to do just the cheek swab?" I paused before attaching the needle to the gold topped vial. "Your last possible exposure was over a year ago."

"Keith, I want to be sure. Really sure." He tapped his antecubital vein with two fingers, improving the target, though it stood up in a ridge behind the tourniquet. His veins looked like fire hoses—I could probably hit one without the tourniquet on, but I understood nerves. The needle punctured his skin; we watched the rich, dark blood well into the vacuum vial as if it contained the secret to the universe. In a way, it did.

Perhaps I should have had Dante draw me first: he was a little awkward with his arm bent over the gauze to stop the bleeding. But he was good as his claim: he slipped into the vein with the needle as deftly as ever he'd slipped into my body. We labeled our samples and marked them STAT, then left the tubes in the lab vault, where a courier would collect them for processing. I shut the vault door and stepped into his embrace.

"Now we wait." He bit his lower lip.

"Dante." I stroked his mouth, trying to get him to release that plump lip from the canines that pressed dents into it. "The results aren't going to change 'forever,' only what we do during our 'forever.'"

That got me a small smile. "Really?"

"Really."

I'm not sure who needed the sex and the holding more that night, me for my grieving, him for his worries, or if we were equally matched because of how I'd suggested turning our lives upside down. I needed to do something to make up for my failure with John. Dante made love to me very slowly, very thoroughly, and sheathed, keeping me face to face, his eyes on mine. He wore me out enough to undo the effect of the nap, letting me sleep dreamlessly in his arms. When I woke extra early the next morning, I started looking for volunteer opportunities, but clicked off the browser before Dante could see the sites I'd pulled up.

"Are you going to be okay to see patients today?" he asked over breakfast.

"I have to be." Swallowing the last of the coffee I was drinking for pleasure and only a little for assistance in keeping my eyes open, I tried to reassure us both. "You can bet I'll be extra vigilant."

We headed downstairs together, and he kissed me goodbye in the waiting room of his first floor clinic. His first patient of the day came in when I went out, carried in a plastic crate by a woman whose face was saying 'aw' as I held the door for her. Guess she saw us through the glass, and it made me happy that someone else, a stranger, could be happy for us. John had needed moments like that.

My day contained no surprises of the patient sort; no one needed an ear or a shoulder for the news I gave them, or for the news they gave me. The printer chattered now and them, spewing out blood counts and protimes, cultures and sensitivities, but not the lab work that mattered most to me. Toward four o'clock, though, two sheets printed off that I practically snatched out of the printer before it finished clattering, and dashed into my office to read behind a closed door.

My heart pounded harder now than it had yesterday during our run. Even though I was quite sure I knew what the results would be, what they should be, I breathed deeply to calm myself, ensuring that I would read what was printed and not what I wanted to see. All the same, I checked twice before I picked up the phone, and again while the hostess wrote down our reservations. Then I called Dante.

"I'm taking you out to dinner," I told him. "Dress nice."

"Ah-hah!" His warm throaty laugh tingled my spine.

"Don't 'ah-hah' me, just put on a jacket." I couldn't blame him for drawing some conclusions, but did he really think I'd take him to some dive diner if the news wasn't good? "A tie only if you want it."

"What time?"

"Seven." I'd tried to allow enough time for a quick shopping trip, and maybe a quickie and/or a shower. "We'll need about twenty minutes travel time."

"I might be a little late, but that should work." He rumbled deep in his throat, a sound I loved to hear. "I'll hurry."

He drew "ah-hah" conclusions and I was left with "huh?" I should have asked if he had surgery scheduled, but he'd have said something if he'd needed to watch an animal's recovery. The last patient I had scheduled left happier than she'd come, because while I tried not to slop my bad moods onto patients, I wasn't nearly so careful with good moods.

Dante wasn't there when I got home, but the cats added their bit of panache to my black slacks, carefully leaving some choice hairs on my legs once I'd dressed. Dante caught me with the sticky lint roller in hand. He was already dressed, looking good in a pale yellow oxford cloth shirt under a navy jacket. If I hadn't planned something special for us, I'd have peeled it all off him then and there.

"Ready?" He held me close, a fine, firm hug, slightly lumpy in a couple of places, and with a bottle of champagne in his hand. Clever man. He parked it in the fridge to chill. "Where are we going?"

"Cassis." I pointed my little Acura toward Boulder.

On the way, Dante placed his hand on my knee and looked at me with serious eyes. "I don't want to spoil your presentation, but—"

"All good." Our dinner wouldn't be the wonderful event I wanted it to be if he was doubting his "ah-hah" conclusion. "You don't mind if I go through with the plans anyway, do you?"

He leaned back against the head rest and closed his eyes, a smile visible in profile. I had to quit looking sideways when we reached the twisty road up Flagstaff Mountain. The elegant restaurant was built into top of the mountain, with three levels overlooking Boulder and Denver. I'd asked to be seated at a window, but somehow I didn't think I'd be admiring the view outside as much as the view across the table.

"I'll enjoy that."

"You like getting romanced, don't you?" This was the man who'd put champagne on ice for later.

"Of course." He squeezed my leg.

I'd keep that in mind for the years to come.

We tried to keep dinner conversation normal, but we both had a tendency to trail off our words and forget our trains of thought, and after the first amazed glance, we didn't really look at the panorama that lay below. If it wasn't our states of mind creating brain cramps, it was the food. My salad of wild greens, garnished with dried fruits and wet walnuts, had a seared *foie gras* on top.

"You aren't supposed to make that noise when I'm not involved," Dante muttered.

I let the morsel on my tongue slide down my throat. "I'm sharing only because I love you." I held out a bite on the end of my fork.

"I see what you mean," he finally came to enough to say. "What is that?"

He probably wouldn't approve of it on humanitarian grounds. "Orgasm on a plate. I'll tell you tomorrow. Tonight, we eat it."

He sat a little straighter. "Don't you think I should know before?"

Dante's shadowy ex-lover said "Trust me," and created the havoc we were still trying to recover from. I might have earned his trust, but I'd done it by being trustworthy. "Goose liver. *Foie gras*."

He went silent, and I could practically hear the gears turning. Then he opened his mouth for another taste, and I was never so glad to share a delicacy. "Do you want half?"

"One more bite. It's pretty rich." He accepted the next morsel with every sign of enjoyment, and I heaved a sigh of relief and ate some frisée lettuce to clear my brain. He had every right to know what he was getting into, even if it was a guilty pleasure sort of food.

"I'm sorry. But people tend to turn it down just from knowing." I did look out the window now, at the shadows that crept down the mountain toward the plains below; the sun was setting to the west, on the other side of the Flatirons.

"You have to know to make a real choice." Dante reached his fork into my plate, but captured one of the wet walnuts.

The entrees were set before us when he asked me, "Any more thoughts on moving to Angola or wherever the need is greatest?"

"Yeah." I sliced off a bite of the polenta with wild mushrooms. "I think I had the right idea but the wrong execution."

"Oh?" Dante invited me to tell him more, but his mouth was full of buffalo tenderloin.

"I have to do something, but there's need much closer to home." The asparagus had been grilled with balsamic vinaigrette—it kept me from giving details for a moment.

"So I don't need to sell the practice after all?" His smile had relief in it, but also humor; his eyes crinkled at the corners.

"No, I'm not going to drag you to the Sudan for a year." I knew a nurse who had done that, and she'd come back full of stories and with a profoundly different understanding of the world.

"If it's only a year, I'd find a *locum tenens*." Dante turned his head suddenly, and I followed his gaze; a trio of deer picked their way across the meadow outside in the dusk. "I wouldn't sell if we were coming back."

I wondered what kind of animal would wander through camp in the Sudan; my nurse friend had mentioned incursions, sometimes by predators. "You were serious about going."

Dante put his fork down and rested his hand over mine. "'Whither thou goest, I go'." His dark eyes held my gaze, giving me the sort of palpitations I wouldn't treat. What kind of response could I make to that? I curled my fingers into his, oblivious of the other diners.

Before I got maudlin, he gave me an extra squeeze and turned his attention back to the food. "So, if not the Sudan or the Philippines, then what?"

"Well, it could be some Third World country, on a short term basis, one of those working vacation things. Go for a week, repair everything you can repair, hit the beach for a couple days after, knowing you did some good in the world." That was still a viable option. "You might do Goat Clinic for a week."

He laughed. "My goat textbook is gathering dust on some high shelf in my office. I'll drag it down."

We finished our meal on a lighter note, declining the luscious offerings on the dessert cart. Instead of going directly back to the car after, I took Dante to the stairs at the edge of the patio. It led us to a veranda outside a banquet room, unused tonight, and a major reason I'd chosen this restaurant. We had a glorious view of the cities laid out below us, glittering in the near dark, matched by the few stars bright enough to show this early. We could hear the other diners as a muffled background, with only the occasional bark of laughter as a distinct sound, and only enough light to see in black and white.

"About that presentation." I pulled the lab reports out of my pocket and offered them. "We are both negative, Dante."

He took the papers but didn't try to read them in the dimness. Tucking them away in his own inner pocket, he looked out over the cities and said nothing. I lay my hand on the small of his back and waited. He'd talk when he was ready.

"And we'll stay that way?" There was a little choke in his voice.

"Yes, we will. If it's only us, we will."

"Then we will." He turned now and drew me against his body. I found his mouth and brushed my lips softly over his, wanting to savor every small texture of him, from his smooth-shaven chin to the damp inside of his lip. We explored each other slowly, carefully, much more carefully than we had the first time we'd ever kissed, ever touched, and if I picked up any momentum at all, we might never be welcome back at this restaurant. That would be a shame, because I'd made a note of the date and figured we'd need an annual reservation. The crisp prickles of his hair, clipped close to his scalp, and the subtle spiciness of his cologne mingling with the scent of his skin were working on my resolve, though, so I pulled back.

"You meant it when you said 'forever,' so yes."

"I meant it." He pulled back a little farther and began hunting in a pocket in the general vicinity of a lump that had been the only drawback to hugging him. His other lumpiness didn't have any sharp corners to it.

The mystery was a small box, which he opened. The contents flashed a small counterpoint to the city lights and the stars. "I had to guess on the size." Dante took my left hand, aimed the ring over the fingertip and repeated his words from earlier. "'Whither thou goest, I go'." He kissed me chastely, the kiss of promise rather than of passion, and I answered it the same.

"I—" Pulling a similar box from my own pocket, I showed it to him. "I had to guess on the size, too. But you just put this ring on me and I want us to match— we'll have to trade it in."

His sudden intake of breath was what I'd hoped to hear. I stuffed the box back in my pocket. "I got two." He found my hand and pressed a ring into it. It was smooth under my touch, domed and rounded, and I meant to put it on him. Sliding it onto Dante's finger, I repeated, "'Whither thou goest, I go'." It slid all the way on—he'd sized his own perfectly. Without releasing his hand, I leaned over and met his lips again, sealing our vow. Then we were tight against each other, and for the second time in two days, we were leaking at the eyes, but these were much happier tears.

"I now pronounce us husband and husband," Dante whispered into my ear.

"Don't I wish." I'd been thinking about destinations where we could make ourselves official.

"It's true. Quirk of Colorado law, left over from the frontier days when there wasn't necessarily an official around to do the ceremony. The couple declares themselves married and it counts. You register it when and if you can." He nuzzled my ear. "'When' will be after some laws get changed, but trust me, this counts. You are officially stuck with me."

"Good!" I wanted to be stuck on him, to start our wedding night. "For an elopement, this could have used a bit more planning." I had a double handful of his butt, taut within his dress slacks.

"We could go back upstairs and have them serve us a slice of that decadent chocolate torte for our wedding cake." Dante suggested. "Or there's champagne at home."

"Home" never sounded more like poetry. We got down Flagstaff Mountain and back in record time.

"Critters, your daddies are home! And we're married!" Dante bellowed at the top of the stairs. The sugar glider swung upside down, chittering, one of the cats opened an eye to say, "Yeah, yeah," and two came to strop their wedding gifts of cat hairs all over us. I reached down to stroke our cats. *Our cats!* We had a lot more organizing to do to get this official.

"Weren't we supposed to carry each other in over the threshold?"

"If you can figure out how we carry each other at the same time, we can try again." Dante rummaged in the kitchen for some wine glasses and set them next to the champagne. "Tell you what, if you want ceremonies, we can invent whatever you like and everybody can sniffle along with us, although I refuse to wear a tuxedo jacket with tails that drag on the ground."

The mental image of that get-up jolted me out of my traditional thinking. "I still think we should have a party. Celebrate with our friends."

"Yeah, that's a good idea. But for now..." Dante twisted the wire cage off the champagne bottle and motioned me to him. "Help me open this."

We held the bottle on the counter between us with one hand each, and used the other hands to wiggle the cork out. The pressure inside the bottle shot the cork out between us, bouncing it off the ceiling and sending it skittering across the floor. A little foam followed the cork, rolling over the lip of the opening and over our hands, christening us as a couple. An unplanned ceremony, but I liked it. "I, too, pronounce us husband and husband." We left our hands on the bottle while we kissed again.

Dante poured for us and handed a glass to me. "To us; to a long and happy life together." We clinked our glasses.

"To us," I agreed, and tasted, skipping the twined arms and trying to feed each other sips without spilling. Getting my mind around suddenly being a married man made me drain that glass faster than might have been strictly wise, but Dante refilled it and led me to the couch.

"Still in shock, Keith?"

"A little." I leaned against his chest, under his arm. We're about the same height until we sit down, because I'm more legs and Dante's more torso. "But glad of it."

"I want you to always be glad of it." He rubbed his cheek against my hair. We sat quietly, drinking the champagne, and then having to laugh, because Harpo and Domino were using the cork for a game of kitty-soccer, batting it back and forth through the living room.

"I have another cat toy for them." I wobbled into the bedroom to find the condom box. Blowing one up like a balloon made Dante do a double take, but then he grabbed another and puffed it to a huge round ball. We flicked the misshapen spheres to the floor, attracting Pawlina's attention, and sat back to enjoy the floor show. Our three cats rolled over, swatting, pouncing, and enjoying the novelty, until someone stuck a claw through the latex. The pop startled the kitties under the couch and brought our attention back to each other.

"Good use for them." Dante slipped one hand into my shirt and his tongue into my mouth. "Since we don't need them any more."

The words turned my legs to rubber. Since my first sexual experiences, the importance of protection had been part of my awareness, had been a controlling factor of my sex life. Now, my partner—*my husband!*—and I could leave that behind. Touch each other without barriers. Pounce on each other without patting pockets or opening drawers first. Or checking the condoms for bite marks.

"Let's go to bed now," I suggested, and Dante escorted me to the bedroom.

We undressed each other with great deliberation, unbuttoning and unzipping, sliding fabric away from flesh in what felt like a ritual, unveiling each other's bodies slowly, on this, our wedding night. He ran his hands over my skin, dark against my paleness, and my own hands were ghosts against his flesh. I knelt to get his trousers off and stole his socks, one at a time, marveling at the beauty of him and that we were pledged. His erection, hard, thick, throbbing, bobbed before my face. I captured it, nearly purple in my hands, clasping his cock but not stroking. A small kiss at the tip, where a bead of moisture had formed, drew a gasp from him and tightened his hand on my shoulder. I'd suck him soon, but for now, admiration. I licked and stood up.

He stripped me the rest of the way and stayed kneeling at my feet, running his hands up and down my legs and over my butt. I stood before my love, wearing nothing but my wedding ring.

"Keith..." Dante cut off his words by pressing his mouth to the side of my cock, holding it to his lips with the palm of his hand, licking a single swipe up to the tip. "I want..." He came to his feet.

"Yes." My husband could have whatever he wanted tonight.

"You haven't even heard." On his feet now, he embraced me, our hard bodies and hard cocks crushed together.

"Doesn't matter, you can have it." My mouth wasn't exactly under my control—I started at his neck and up his chin, pausing at his mouth to stroke his chin, then his lips, and across to find his little flat ear. His hands flexed against my ass, parting my cheeks and pulling me against his cock.

"Let me top again tonight." His voice was husky, the words nearly a growl.

"Yes."

"Oh, Keith..." He thrust his mouth into the bend of my neck and bit, hard enough there might be a bruise. "I've been wanting..."

"We could have before." I would have toppled us both onto the bed without any more talking, but he wasn't done.

"No. I had to be sure. Really sure." He found my earlobe and sucked. "Now I am. Sure of you. Sure you love me."

"I love you, you ass." Maybe that wasn't mushy but it was honest. "I've never gone bareback, either way." And if he didn't stop talking, that wasn't going to change soon enough for me. I pulled us both over onto the bed and wrapped my legs around him.

"Eager little bottom, are you?" He nipped my ear. "Slow down, this is important."

"Speed up a little, this is important." I wanted him, *now*. "Lube, Dante."

"Okay, okay." He reached into the drawer for the bottle. "Roll over."

On my belly and with legs spread, I waited for the cold drizzle of slickness, which he worked into my hole with two fingers. His other arm held me from below and his cheek lay hot against my skin. His hips weren't still—his cock pressed rhythmically against my leg. "I'm probably not gonna last long," he admitted to my back.

"Dante, please, just..." The need was going to overwhelm me soon. "Will you please just get started?" His hand left my ass and finally stroked more lube onto his shaft; I could feel the bumping against my leg.

At last he was a warm pressure against my crack, heated hips against my butt, and then oh, a welcome fullness in my ass, sliding in, opening me, widening me with his flesh. Pausing with just the head inside, he waited until I nodded, pressing up and in, giving me his whole thickness. At last, we touched and there was no barrier, no separation, our most intimate skins rubbed together, and when he did come, he left his warmth within me. I left mine everywhere: Dante rolled us to our sides without uncoupling and wrapped his hand around my shaft for the few strokes it took to bring me to climax. I didn't want to move; his lips lay against my neck. Our rings clinked, a tiny metallic cheer, when I wrapped my fingers into his. My ring was a bit loose; we'd get it sized later.

"I love you, Dante." I brought his knuckles to my mouth for a tiny nibble that didn't last long—sleep was sucking at me.

"Love you, too, Keith." He pulled out but didn't roll over, only pulled the sheet over us. "And you're gonna wake up in the morning and still be married to me."

We woke up Saturday morning and made love again, this time with me topping. I was perfectly content to spend the rest of my life figuring out which way I liked it better. Well, bare. I liked it best bare, with Dante, in a life that rolled out with possibilities.

He asked me about them, once we were up and dressed. "So are we going to go repair cleft palates in Mexico for our honeymoon?"

"Mmm, no. I think we plan a trip just for us first." I pulled him away from his coffee cup for a kiss. "The cleft palate thing needs some coordination."

"You aren't giving up the idea?" Dante had brought the textbook on goats upstairs already and had indeed wiped away a thick layer of dust.

"No, not at all, but for doing something concrete, in John's memory, I thought...I'll probably need a couple of classes, but that isn't impossible, the metro area is brimming with resources." I drained my coffee and considered a third cup plus some aspirin —two glasses of champagne last night had gone slightly to my head and the prospect of mowing our lawn loomed. "But I think I should do some sort of outreach, or support for teens. Do what John needed way before he got to my office. Then I'd have a better shot of accomplishing something truly useful."

"Is this instead of or in addition to your practice?"

"In addition to. Part of." I stood up and came to rub his shoulders. "I won't do anything drastic without discussion, Dante. Except start the lawnmower this morning."

He winced. "Might as well get it over with. And I need to get downstairs and flip the sign; someone's waiting in their car."

"Happy vetting." I leaned down to rub my lips against his hair. "I'll go mow."

But the person in the car wasn't there to see Dante.

The young man came to stand at the gate, watching me trundle out the mower. He didn't come in until I was almost ready to pull the cord and start the engine, and then I paused, unwilling to drown out what he might say.

"Are you Dr. Hoyer?" He tried to meet my eyes a couple of times, but he seemed fixated on the golden ring glittering on my hand. He looked familiar; I might have seen him recently and thought I knew where.

"I am. What can I do for you?" He looked like he was about sixteen or seventeen. That he was standing in the sunshine, breathing, sent a pang through me for a young man who would never do those things again.

"I was a friend of John Carsten's," he said softly. "Do you need your lawn mowed?"

I left him with the machine and went inside to make some iced tea.

About the Author

P.D. Singer lives in Colorado with her slightly bemused husband, two rowdy teenage boys, and thirty pounds of cats. She's a big believer in research, first-hand if possible, so the reader can be quite certain PD has skied down a mountain face-first, been stepped on by rodeo horses, acquired a potato burn or two, and will never, ever, write a novel that includes sky-diving.

When not writing, playing her fiddle, or skiing, she can be found with a book in hand. Her husband blesses the advent of ebooks — they're staving off the day the house collapses from the weight of the printed page.

Pam is always glad to hear from readers; feel free to send a note to PD.Singer@rockyridgebooks.com or hunt up the news at http://PDSinger.com.

Other books by P.D. Singer
    Fire on the Mountain
    Snow on the Mountain
    Fall Down the Mountain
    Blood on the Mountain
    Return to the Mountain
    The Rare Event
    Spokes
    Donal *agus* Jimmy
    Prep Work
    O'Carolan's Seduction
    Tail Slide (also available as Slip/Slide/Snow in the anthology Out in Colorado)

More from Rocky Ridge Books:

From Eden Winters
    Diversion
    Corruption
    Manipulation
    Summer Boys
    The Match Before Christmas
    Fanning the Flames
    A Lie I can Live With
    Match for the Holidays (contains The Match Before Christmas, Fanning the Flames, and A Lie I Can Live With)
    Tinsel and Frost
    Highway Man
    Almost Mine

From Cari Z
    Wanting More (with bonus story Favorite Dish)

From Z. Allora
    With Wings (Dark Angels Book 1)
    Tied Together (Dark Angles Book 2)
    Finally Fallen (Dark Angels Book 3)
    Happy Holidays (Dark Angels 4)